Short Story Collection

And yet
He Married
Her

UMM
ZAKIYYAH

And Yet He Married Her: Short Story Collection
by Umm Zakiyyah

Copyright © 2025 by Al-Walaa Publications
All Rights Reserved.

ISBN: 978-1-942985-21-1

UZ Books available at:
uzauthor.com • **uzhearthub.com** • **uzuniversity.com**

Order inquires: **wholesale@ummzakiyyah.com**

Published by Al-Walaa Publications
Dallas, Texas USA

TABLE OF CONTENTS

AUTHOR'S NOTE

In this fiction collection, I share three short stories about religious and emotional trauma as manifested in the lives of Muslim women and youth. *Dance of Serenity* is a three-part story of religious and emotional trauma in the context of a challenging marriage. *Who Am I?* is a four-part story of emotional trauma as incited by a challenging friendship between teens. *Drowning Beneath Her Feet* is a five-part story of religious and emotional trauma in the context of a parent-child relationship.

Although I tend to use innuendo more than explicit exploration of emotionally wounding experiences, some of the themes might be triggering or emotionally challenging for readers, especially for survivors of trauma or abuse, or for highly sensitive persons.

So, dear reader, if for any reason you find yourself triggered or emotionally dysregulated as you read the fictional scenes from these stories, I encourage you to pause and do breathwork and/or journaling. Or simply step away for a moment (or for however long you need) until your inner world feels calm and safe enough to continue reading.

It is my hope that these short stories are thought-provoking and enjoyable to read, and that they inspire deep discussions amongst friends, book clubs, and fellow readers.

For any Arabic words for which the context doesn't make immediately clear, I encourage readers to do a quick online search for the meaning in lieu of a dedicated glossary in the book.

For every hurting heart and struggling soul who is turning their pain into power

"There is no greater agony than bearing an untold story inside you."
— Maya Angelou, *I Know Why the Caged Bird Sings*

Dance of Serenity

a three-part short story

*"There are places our spirits feel at ease,
no matter how austere, just as there are places
we cannot call home, no matter how opulent..."*
—Ross Story's diary, *The Last Promise*
by Richard Paul Evans

PART ONE

Songs of the Spirit

1

Laughter crawled in Sakinah's throat as she swayed her hips and moved her shoulders rhythmically to Whitney Houston's "I'm Every Woman." In the wall-to-wall mirror of the dance studio in the basement of her home, Sakinah saw a grin toying at one side of her mouth.

"You are the most narcissistic person I know," her elder sister Kaida would often say. "I don't know anyone else who gets so much pleasure from just looking in the mirror."

When Sakinah was in high school, Kaida's teasing comments would sting, and Sakinah sometimes felt ashamed of herself. Was it wrong that her greatest joy was spending time alone in front of the mirror? Was it wrong to enjoy looking at herself?

But Sakinah wasn't just *looking* at herself. She was studying the fluid movements of her arms and legs, the ribbed firmness of her torso, and how when she moved one part of her body, the others followed as if in submission. It was a soulful, rhythmic chant of the limbs, a language that emanated from the soul and traveled the course of her body until she bellowed a wordless song that some would call *dance*.

But this language of movement was more than dance. It was a spirited cry of healing. And it ran so deep that her arms and legs, and hands and feet sometimes, ached from exorcising the physical and emotional toxins from within.

This inebriation is what took hold of Sakinah and kept her transfixed in front of the mirror for sometimes hours at a time. Even now, as Whitney Houston sang, "It's all in meeeee," the reflection captured a most striking display of human beauty. Yes, it was Sakinah's body that spoke the wordless language of the spirit that held Sakinah's attention right then. But it was not Sakinah herself whom Sakinah was in awe of as joy threatened to escape in the form of laughter from her throat. It was God.

How immeasurably magnificent her Creator was, Sakinah thought at that moment. It was Allah—*Al-Musawwir*—who had perfectly shaped and designed the indescribable beauty of the feminine form. She was captivated and humbled, and ever so grateful to be divinely gifted a female body to carry her soul through this transient world.

"...one is abhorrent, and the other is criminal."

The words floated into Sakinah's consciousness as if from a distance, and it took a moment for Sakinah to realize that the sound was coming from the widescreen television affixed to a wall of the basement. Sakinah stopped dancing, remembering suddenly why she had both the television and music on at the same time. She rushed toward the remote control and lifted it from where it lay on the floor in front of the wall-to-wall mirror. Sakinah pointed the remote toward the massive stereo system, silencing Whitney Houston's voice mid-sentence, the sound now replaced by voices coming from the television.

"But, Dr. Gordon, how do you draw the line?" The middle-aged white man with streaks of gray in his dark hair leaned forward slightly from the comfort of the chair he occupied each week to interview famous athletes, singers, actors, and authors. "If we condone any form of physical discipline," he said, "then certainly we're condoning all physical abuse."

Sakinah was breathing heavily from the intense dance workout as she settled on the hardwood floor. She folded her legs pretzel style in front of her as she used the television remote to turn up the volume. Perspiration beaded her forehead and slipped down her temples. She glanced around for a towel before realizing she'd left her workout towel upstairs in her bedroom. She wiped her head with the flat of her hand then rubbed the moisture on her black yoga pants as she turned her attention back to the television.

"That's a very difficult question to answer," Dr. Gordon replied. His hair too was graying, and he and the host appeared to be about the same age. But Dr. Gordon's skin was a deep bronze brown and his hair a closely cropped salt-and-pepper afro.

Sakinah could see the book *The Abuse of Abuse* by Dr. Hakim Gordon lying on the small table between the two chairs before the host lifted it and opened it to a page he'd tabbed.

"Physical abuse is a criminal act that must be punishable by law," the host read aloud from Dr. Gordon's book. *"But physical punishment is an abhorrent disciplinary strategy that must be corrected by parenting classes and therapy if necessary."*

The host set the book back down. "Would you say this is your definition of the line between physical abuse and spanking?"

"No," Dr. Gordon said, his deep voice rising authoritatively even as he remained composed. "That is my professional assessment of the best way to treat the two. Defining a clear line between the two requires a much more intensive analysis and explanation."

"But isn't it simpler to merely draw the line at physical violence itself?" the host asked skeptically. "If we outlaw all hitting, wouldn't our tax dollars be saved from this costly analysis you're suggesting?"

"Yes," Dr. Gordon replied with an agreeable nod. But Sakinah detected the almost imperceptible grin creasing one side of her father's lips. "But only if your goal is to save money and time," he said. "Mine is to save families and children."

After the talk show, Sakinah hurried up the hardwood steps and turned the handle of the door that led out of the basement. She wanted to take a shower and prepare for her own television interview. Though it wasn't until the following week and was certainly not on a popular television network like her father's, Sakinah wanted to look over the interview questions the hostess had emailed her last night. She still struggled with nervousness in front of cameras if she was doing anything other than dancing or singing. Besides, it was Friday and she would be busy this weekend and early next week with Songs of the Spirit meetings, rehearsals, and paperwork, so this evening was probably the last time she would have to prepare for the talk show.

Sakinah was smiling to herself as she stepped into the kitchen and closed the door to the basement. Her father had managed to inject a small plug for her company after the host had challenged him on the premise of the book's chapter "All Hurt Doesn't Harm."

"It's about being alert to the needs and limits of your individual children," her father had told the host, "just like we need to be alert to the needs and limits of our individual bodies."

Then her father immediately added, "For example, when my daughter is training dancers for her troupe at Songs of the Spirit, she tells them if they want the intense workout sessions to adequately prepare them to be professional dancers, they'll need to know the difference between hurt that strengthens and hurt that harms."

Sakinah had grinned widely at the television screen at that moment, pride and joy swelling in her chest. "And that's what parents need to do," Dr. Gordon said, a smile toying at his lips that Sakinah knew was especially for her.

"And yes, I do respect your view that it's best to nip physical abuse in the bud by outlawing all physical discipline," her father said. "But in my professional opinion, that's about as sensible as nipping verbal abuse in the bud by outlawing all use of our vocal cords in corrective discipline."

2

"Hey, Sakinah," a deep voice said. Sakinah looked up from where she was sitting on her living room couch, and her heart raced in excitement and desire upon seeing Daryl standing opposite her. His brown skin was the color of rich honey, and his muscle-toned arms shined of fresh perspiration in the fitted, sleeveless workout shirt he wore.

"Hey, Daryl," Sakinah said softly, closing the book she was reading. "What are you—"

"Hey, Sakinah!"

Sakinah's eyes fluttered open and her heart raced as someone firmly grasped her shoulder and shook her. Fahim's expression was contorted, thinning patience written in the deep brown folds of his forehead.

"It's time for Fajr," he said, releasing his grip.

Though still distracted by the dream, Sakinah could see her husband's tightened jaw beneath the beginnings of the beard he hadn't shaved in weeks. Or maybe it had been months now. She'd lost count.

Sakinah's eyes lingered momentarily on the coils of hair that faded into thin patches on his shirtless chest, and she fought the urge to pull Fahim toward her and hold him close right then.

"What time is it?" Sakinah rubbed her eyes and sat up on her elbows, the covers falling from her shoulders to reveal the spaghetti straps of her black night gown.

Fahim frowned. "I'm going to the masjid, so I won't be able to take Malik to his game."

"What?" Sakinah tossed the covers away from her body and swung her legs over the edge of the bed until her bare feet rested on the soft carpet. "He's expecting you to be there."

"Then *you* take him. I'm busy today."

"Fahim, you can't do this to him."

"You mean, I can't do this to *you*?" Fahim angrily pulled a hooded sweatshirt over his head and pushed his arms through the sleeves. "Malik will be fine," Fahim said as he tugged at the lower hem of his hoodie until it was straightened just below his waist. "Let's see if quality time with your son is more important than sipping coffee with strange men while you pretend to talk about business."

Sakinah's face contorted in offense. "What's that supposed to mean?"

"I'll let you figure that out," Fahim said as he grabbed his car keys from the dresser and started for the door. "But for now, I have to pray."

Sakinah stood and followed him, the hem of her silk night gown falling to her thighs. "You can't just say something like that and walk out. I've never done anything inappropriate during my meetings."

"Oh yeah?" Fahim did not turn around. "Wearing revealing clothes? Putting on make-up and perfume?"

"You put on nice clothes and cologne when you go to work." Sakinah followed him down the hall. "I never accused you of flirting."

Fahim turned around to face his wife before descending the stairs. "I'm a man, Sakinah. I can wear nice clothes and cologne if I want. It's the Sunnah."

"And it's the Sunnah for women to be ugly and stink?"

Fahim threw up a hand as he turned around and started down the steps. "Study your religion, Sakinah. Then we can talk."

"You mean study from Saudi sheikhs?" she called out from the top of the steps. "No thank you. The extremists

15

have caused Arab women enough havoc. I'm American, and I'm not signing up for it."

"Then sign up for Islam." Fahim raised his voice as he disappeared from view.

"*As-salaamu'alaikum*," he said with finality. "Don't wait up for me."

Seconds later, Sakinah heard the front door close, and the only sound that remained was her angry breaths.

The distant chime of a cell phone came from the direction of her room, and Sakinah immediately recognized the familiar ring tone. Sakinah sighed as she retreated down the hall, annoyed that Fahim had left his phone at home, again. Sakinah was starting to wonder if he was leaving it on purpose so she wouldn't be able to reach him.

The cell phone chimed and vibrated on the nightstand until Sakinah silenced it before collapsing into bed on her back. She needed to gather her thoughts before preparing for prayer.

Sakinah nibbled at her lower lip as she realized she would have to cancel her business meeting that morning because of Malik's soccer game.

Why was Fahim doing this? He had agreed to keep Malik today, and she was going to take Zaynah to her parents' house so she could attend her business meeting.

Should she just take them both to her parents?

The thought incited anxiety. Her parents would naturally be happy to keep both Malik and Zaynah, but that would mean Malik would miss the soccer game. Sakinah couldn't in good conscience ask her parents to take Malik to his game, at least not without a good explanation as to why Fahim wasn't taking him as planned. Sakinah was not in the mood to defend her marriage life today. But she doubted she could, even if she wanted to. She was having trouble understanding it herself.

If only her parents knew that their daughter was hanging on by a thread living with Fahim these last two years. It took everything in Sakinah to keep from complaining to her mother and father, but she knew that Fahim would never forgive her if she did. And maybe she'd never forgive herself.

Fahim was a good man, after all. Sakinah just needed to be patient with her marital struggles, she kept telling herself. It was only natural to go through challenges after nine years of marriage, and Sakinah wasn't about to give up now. She didn't want her children to live in a broken home. Besides, she really wanted her marriage to be "happily ever after," or at least some semblance of it. She wanted to one day look back on thirty plus years of marriage, as her parents were able to do.

The vibrating of Fahim's phone made Sakinah groan as she sat up and headed toward the bathroom in her master bedroom to prepare for Fajr prayer.

At the marble sink, Sakinah turned the brass knobs one at a time and placed her right palm under the steady stream. The shock of cold water made her flinch, and her mind conjured up the image of Fahim's twisted expression as he called her a whore for not giving up dancing and singing in public.

"Do you have any idea how you make me look?" he'd said to her a few weeks ago right before she left for a sold-out performance at Howard University. She could feel his hot, angry breaths in her face. "All the brothers at the masjid think I'm some emasculated punk for letting my wife shake her ass in front of men."

"How do they even know what I'm doing?" she shot back. "If they're so holy, they shouldn't be watching."

"They watch because you want them to."

The now warm water pooled in Sakinah's palm and ran like thin rivers between the gaps in her fingers. Sakinah slowly closed her eyes in sadness and self-rebuke, and the image of Daryl's mouth on hers appeared in her mind. Her eyes shot open, and her breath caught in desire and shame. But she could not slow the rapid pulse or calm the inflammation of warmth she felt in her limbs.

Sakinah stared at the face staring back at her, wide-eyed and pitiful. Her expression was a cross between wanting to cry and uncertainty that it was even worth it. She was like a child who'd fallen down and wanted someone to notice but was shocked that no one did.

"I like your baby hair," Daryl had said that fateful day, running a single finger along the kinky curls of her hairline. Immediately, Sakinah's hand had self-consciously gone to her frayed thick braids, as if protecting them from his gaze, and from her own shame. She hadn't groomed herself for him. How could she have? She hadn't known she would need to.

Sakinah's chin trembled at the memory, and the reflection of her untamed mass of kinky curls only made the recollection more tormenting. She cursed herself for not being able to let go of it. It had been ten years since she scrambled out the back door of Daryl's home and rushed back to school on legs that ached so badly that she wondered from whence she gathered the strength to walk. But she had ignored her aching limbs and groin as her heart pounded in trepidation that she wouldn't make it in time to meet her younger brother when the last bell rang.

"I'm going to marry Fahim," she'd told Daryl three weeks later, a month before they both graduated from high school.

"What the f—" he had said.

But Sakinah had covered his mouth with her hand before he could finish. "Daryl!" she'd shouted in shock, stupidly looking around to see if anyone had heard him though there was no one in his living room except Sakinah and Daryl himself.

Presently, the sound of birds chirping outside reminded Sakinah that she still hadn't prayed the dawn prayer. She bowed her head and spread the water over her hands then brought a handful to her mouth and nose to start *wudhoo*, the ritual ablution before Salaah, the Muslim formal prayer.

After praying, Sakinah sat on the thick softness of the prayer mat in her room, her heart heavy in sadness and confusion. But she felt resolute that she needed to make some changes in her life.

Maybe Fahim was right when he said she wanted men to watch her. Because there was one man her heart would not release her from.

Each time she danced or was under the blaring lights of a television studio or sat in front of a massive camera, she wondered if Daryl was watching. Sakinah wondered if Daryl was haunted, in sleep and wakefulness, by the image of them clinging breathlessly to each other. Two teenage honor students skipping school.

In that fateful moment together, they had been utterly shocked that no chemistry lesson could explain the fiery eruption of their hearts. Pain and pleasure had exploded inside Sakinah until she'd wept—whether from happiness or shame, she didn't know. But Daryl had held her tighter, and she'd laid her head on his chest and wondered how she would tell her parents she wanted to marry the valedictorian, whose father was an active member of the interfaith Muslim-Christian initiative that her father, Dr. Hakim Gordon, spearheaded.

The shrilling of the house phone made Sakinah start, and she turned to look toward the nightstand to see if she could make out the number on the cordless caller identification screen. "Unavailable" it read, and Sakinah sighed as she turned back around and mentally drowned out the annoying ring.

Sakinah's thoughts drifted to what Fahim had said about her need to study her religion, and anxiety knotted in her chest. She couldn't bring herself to want to. Everyone she'd known who had taken up the task, she was no longer in contact with. They became so distant and cold. They'd behaved as if every conversation was an opportunity to tell her everything that was wrong with her life. She didn't wear hijab properly. She shouldn't listen to music. She shouldn't sing or dance in public. The wealth she was earning from her business was *haraam*, cursed and forbidden.

Sakinah couldn't recall a single positive result of someone "studying the religion."

"Nobody needs to *study* Islam," Hakim would often say, indignant. "We need to live it and learn it. In that order."

In the quiet of her thoughts, Sakinah grunted agreement with her father. What was the point of "studying Islam" anyway?

"Just think about it, Sakinah," one of her former acquaintances-turned-religious had said years ago. "Living in this non-Muslim environment desensitizes us. We start to think and act like they do, and it corrupts our hearts until we don't even *want* what's good for us."

Of all the self-righteous rants Sakinah had heard over the years, this was the only statement that gave her pause. The young woman's words had penetrated Sakinah's conscience until Sakinah felt powerless to offer a rebuttal. How could she, when the very heart she'd be defending still pined for a forbidden lover to whom she'd willingly given her chastity? And even the repeated intimacy of her faithful Muslim husband paled in comparison to the fiery pleasure she'd felt that single day she had given into carnal sin.

There was a soft knock at her room door.

"Malik, is that you?" Sakinah called out. "The door's unlocked."

The door opened just enough for Sakinah to see her sleepy son's face.

"Mommy, someone's on the phone for Daddy," Malik's groggy voice said.

Sakinah groaned. How many times had she told Malik not to answer the phone unless she asked him to?

"Okay, honey," she said. "I'll get it. Thank you."

"You're welcome," Malik said as he disappeared behind the closing door.

Sakinah pushed herself to a standing position and walked over to the nightstand and picked up the phone. "Hello?" she said in the politest voice she could muster, trying to hide her annoyance at receiving a call early Saturday morning.

There was a distinct pause, and Sakinah's senses were heightened in suspicion. "Hello?"

"Hello, Mrs. Mitchell?" a woman's voice said.

"Yes..." Sakinah's voice was cordial but cautious.

"My name is Yolanda," the woman said, stumbling briefly at the sound of Malik hanging up the other phone, "and I'm calling from Riyadh, Saudi Arabia, about the teaching post Fahim applied for through our online service."

Sakinah blinked repeatedly. "Excuse me?"

"Is he available?"

"No," Sakinah said, hopefully not too brusquely. "He's not in right now. May I take a message?"

"Can you ask him to call Yolanda from Saudi University Connect?"

"What is your contact number?"

"He has it already," Yolanda said, humor in her tone. "We've been playing phone tag for over a week."

In an effort to appear cordial, Sakinah forced herself to cough laughter. "I'll give him the message."

"Please," Yolanda said. "He's not answering his mobile phone either, and I need an answer by today if possible."

"I'll be sure to let him know."

"Thank you, Mrs. Mitchell."

"And thank you, Yolanda," Sakinah said, talking in a fake, overly courteous tone.

Sakinah nearly slammed the phone down. No, she was not going to cancel a single meeting today. She was going to take Zaynah *and* Malik to her parents' house and let Fahim take the heat for putting his wife and son in this predicament.

PART TWO
And Yet He Married Her

3

"And after this short commercial break," the hostess said, looking into the camera, a wide smile on her face, "we'll be back with Sakinah Gordon-Mitchell, founder and CEO of Songs of the Spirit, the interfaith chorus and dance troupe that is taking the world by storm."

Music played, and the hostess's smile broke after a few seconds, and Sakinah released her own smile then exhaled. The magazine that the hostess had been holding now lay on the table, and the glossy cover showed the poised body of Sakinah with her arms outstretched and head held high just beneath the SW logo for *Successful Women*.

"Do you have to prostitute yourself for fame?" Fahim had asked angrily a week before.

Anxiety tightened in Sakinah's chest as she saw the photo through her husband's eyes. The deep brown of her face was turned slightly to the right to reveal the mole on her neck, and the way the magazine image had been touched up made her skin exude a rich smoothness that suggested that Sakinah's complexion was flawless. The white dance dress she wore in the photo, though modest by industry standards, hugged and accentuated her shapely form, revealing only the skin of her face, neck, and hands, all of which glowed unnaturally—and beautifully—on the glossy page.

"Can we have some water?" The hostess waved a stack of notecards at the glass-enclosed room beyond the camera, the red of her carefully manicured nails flickering briefly. "These lights are scorching."

Seconds later, a man appeared with two small bottles of water and set them on the table in front of the women. The hostess reached for hers and opened the cap, a half smile developing on her face. "You must be hot in all of that. I don't know how you people do it."

The sides of Sakinah's mouth creased in an effort at forced politeness, but she couldn't manage more than that. The words "you people" stung, and Sakinah fought the urge to make an equally offensive comment. Sakinah imagined that the woman wouldn't appreciate the same words being used in reference to Latino-Americans, or even Catholics.

Sakinah absentmindedly ran a hand over the cloth of her black head cover that was tied into a tight bun at the back of her neck. "We manage," she said, smirking almost imperceptibly. "It's not too much different from wearing clothes actually."

The hostess's eyebrows shot up in interest, apparently oblivious to the sarcastic undertone of Sakinah's words. The hostess took a few gulps of water then set the bottle back on the table. "Really? I never thought of it like that."

Sakinah managed a tacit affirmation of cordiality as she reached for her own water bottle. She remained silent as she removed the cap and took a few sips.

"We're back on in thirty seconds," a man called out from behind the camera.

The hostess motioned with her notecards again, waving the man back over. "Can you take these plastic bottles? They make us look like a minority station in Baltimore City."

There were ripples of laughter from the set. It took a moment for Sakinah to realize that the statement was meant as a joke—because the television station was indeed located in a minority-owned studio in inner-city Baltimore.

Discomfort pinched Sakinah as she took another quick sip of water. She quickly handed the nearly full bottle back to the man instead of acknowledging the hostess's humor. Sakinah didn't know if laughter would make her appear sociable or judgmental.

It wasn't until she was on the Baltimore-Washington Parkway driving back toward her home in Potomac, Maryland, that she realized that her silence probably made her appear worse than what she had been trying to avoid.

Sakinah's mobile phone vibrated next to her. She glanced to her side to check the caller ID display before pressing the button on the wire of the earpiece that was already in her right ear.

"*As-salaamu'alaikum*," Sakinah said, using the greeting of peace that was customary amongst Muslims.

"*Wa'alaikumussalaam*, baby. How's my superstar? I know you made me proud."

Sakinah's spirits lifted at the sound of her father's voice. "I'm not sure about that. But they were happy to have me."

"Of course, they were happy to have you. Your interview is giving them ratings. I hope Oprah is next."

Sakinah coughed laughter. "I don't think Oprah knows I exist. Or cares."

"Sakinah, baby," her father said in a gentle scold as his tone grew more serious, "I told you don't do that. Oprah needs you more than you need her. Don't forget that."

Sakinah sighed, but she didn't respond. There was no use. Her father thought she could wow the world. She wondered why she herself wasn't so convinced.

"How many successful African-American female entrepreneurs do you think are even out there, baby?"

"Loads, I'm sure," Sakinah said. "We just don't know them."

"Muslim ones?" Hakim said.

"I know a few."

"Millionaires?"

Sakinah felt the beginning of a headache. No matter how many times Hakim said it, she couldn't get used to it. Yes, her company had grossed over a million dollars for more than three years in a row, but Sakinah didn't think of herself as a millionaire. Besides, after taxes and paying her employees, overhead costs, monthly bills, and her children's private school education, she took home considerably less than half of her company's earnings.

"And stop living in denial," Hakim said. "If you hadn't bought your house and cars in cash, you'd have a lot more than you do now."

"Daddy," Sakinah sighed, "we already talked about this..."

"Yes, and I'm going to talk about it again. I don't like to see young people wasting money like that. There's a reason this country gives us the option for mortgages and car notes."

"Fahim and I don't want to live in debt." She intentionally avoided mentioning the word *ribaa*, knowing the topic of usury was a sore spot in the relationship between her and her father.

"No," Hakim said, his firm tone letting her know that her father had heard exactly what she didn't say. "Fahim is just listening to all that foolishness those foreign Muslims are selling him, and you're playing along."

"Daddy—"

"No, Sakinah, baby, listen to me. I'm telling you this because I love you. All these people do is come to this country to line their pockets and piss on us. They don't care anything about you or your soul. They do whatever the hell they want, and they sell that B.S. to you."

"But, Da—"

"And, trust me, they won't leave you alone until you're walking downtown wearing a black tent over your head, and all your kids are starving. For the sake of Allah," he added sarcastically. "And you know what I'm tal—"

The sound of a beep interrupted her father midsentence.

"Daddy, that's Fahim calling."

"Okay, baby," Hakim said after a hesitant pause, exhaustion in his voice. "Call me when you get home."

"Okay, I will."

"I love you, baby."

"I love you too, Daddy."

At the silencing of the line, Sakinah yanked the wire from her ear and tossed the headset to the empty passenger seat next to her. Sakinah's phone continued to vibrate over and over as Fahim's name and picture appeared on the mobile screen. But Sakinah wasn't in the mood to talk.

With her free hand, Sakinah rummaged through her handbag next to her until she located her iPod and connected the USB cable to the AUX port in her Mercedes. Immediately, the uplifting music of the band Leftist filled the car.

4

Fahim laughed along with the congregation of about twenty brothers who were sitting on the carpeted floor of the men's *musallaa* listening to the imam's short talk after Fajr prayer.

"That's how it is with women," the imam said, toying with his large, greying beard, a jovial smile on his face. "You have to let them know who's in charge." There were emphatic nods in the crowd. "But *nicely*," the imam said jokingly.

The men laughed, and some slapped each other on the shoulder in agreement.

"So instead of kicking her you-know-what to make her do what you want," he said, "kiss her wherever she likes, then tell her what you need her to do."

The men erupted in laughter, and the imam laughed too.

A second later, the imam glanced at his wristwatch. "I think it's getting late, brothers," he said. "I don't want any more of your wives calling me complaining than there are already."

The laughter faded as the imam recited the closing supplication praising Allah and asking His forgiveness, signaling the end of the short talk. "*Subhaanak Allaahumma wa bihamdika, ash-hadu an laa ilaaha illaa ant. Astaghfiruka wa atoobu ilayk.*"

"Sheikh?" Fahim waved his hand to get the imam's attention as the imam got to his feet and Fahim followed suit.

The imam looked in Fahim's direction and nodded. "Yes, Brother Fahim."

"Can I ask you a question?"

"Certainly."

Fahim was only vaguely aware of the small crowd of brothers lingering in the *musallaa* while the others left to put on their shoes and leave the masjid.

"My wife is a singer and a dancer, but—"

The imam closed his eyes in disapproval and muttered a prayer aloud asking Allah to guide her and forgive her.

"—she doesn't believe it's wrong. I want to make *hijrah* to a Muslim country so that our children don't take her lifestyle as an example, but I don't know how to convince her to leave America. She's not really religious or anything, so I doubt she'd ever see the harm in living in a *kaafir* country. She thinks America is more Islamic than Muslim lands."

There was a thoughtful pause.

"Was she a singer and a dancer when you married her?"

Fahim was taken aback by the question. "Yes..." There was uncertainty and shame in the confession. "But not like she is now," he added quickly, hoping to underscore how desperate his situation was.

"Then you have to be patient with her until Allah guides her," the imam said.

Fahim started to protest, but the imam continued speaking before he could.

"You can try to convince her to make *hijrah*," the imam said diplomatically, "as we're commanded to do when we fear for our souls. But you must know that this will not necessarily solve the problem. Muslim countries have many clubs, music, and concerts for people who don't want to live like Muslims."

"Even in Saudi Arabia?"

The imam's eyebrows rose in surprise. "You are thinking to move to Saudi Arabia?"

Fahim couldn't tell if the imam was impressed or displeased. "Yes, sheikh, I am. I've been applying for some jobs there, but I haven't heard anything definite yet."

"You know, life is very difficult for women there," the imam said. "Egypt is probably a better choice."

"Have you lived there, sheikh?"

The imam laughed. "I am from Egypt, my son. I lived there until I was a teenager."

"I meant Saudi Arabia."

The imam frowned slightly. "No. I've only gone for Hajj and Umrah," he said. "But I have family who has lived there for many years."

Fahim's expression brightened. "Really? Are they there now?"

"Yes. I think they consider it home."

"So they like it?"

"Very much."

"I'm sorry, sheikh," Fahim said, eagerness in his tone. "I know this might be too much to ask, but do you think they can help me move my family there?"

The imam drew in a deep breath and rubbed his beard thoughtfully. "You know, son, the visa situation there is very difficult. The Saudis do not like bringing foreigners into the country except for work."

"I'm willing to work. That's what I'm trying to do."

The imam shook his head. "I don't mean it like this, son. What I mean is they don't like people coming with plans to stay. They bring people there to serve them, then when the people are finished their work, they ask them to leave."

"But you said your family has lived there for some time."

"But it hasn't been easy. Most of their wives and children are still in Egypt."

Fahim nodded thoughtfully, unsure what to say. But his mind was set on having any connection to someone in Saudi Arabia, especially an Arab.

"My wife wants to make *hijrah* too," someone said.

Fahim turned to see a young bearded man who appeared to be of Pakistani decent approaching the imam.

"She wants to live in Riyadh," the Pakistani man said.

"Then I think you two should talk," the imam said, laughing heartily. He shook their hands and gave them salaams.

"Excuse me," the imam said as he headed for the double doors of the *musallaa*, "but I have to run. I promised my wife I won't spend *all* morning in the masjid," he said lightheartedly. "*Inshaa'Allah*, I'll see you later today."

5

The imam disappeared behind a slowly closing door as Abbas looked after him.

"Your wife really wants to move to Saudi Arabia?"

Abbas turned his attention to the African-American brother standing next to him. The man's eyes were aglow with admiration and hopefulness, and Abbas felt a tinge of guilt for being unable to share those feelings.

"Yes." Abbas chuckled in discomfort. "She's been on me about it for the last few months."

"*Maashaa'Allah.*" The brother smiled and shook his head as he reached out a hand to Abbas while uttering the Arabic expression that literally meant, *God willed it*. But socially, it really meant, *That's amazing*.

"I'm Fahim, by the way," the man added as Abbas accepted the handshake.

"Abbas."

"Maybe our wives should get together," Fahim said. "I'd love for my wife to meet some real Muslims."

Abbas drew his eyebrows together, an awkward smile forming on his face. "Real Muslims?"

Fahim laughed. "She's not the masjid type, so she doesn't come around Muslims much."

"Well, she is a woman, you know."

Fahim's expression was a mixture of humor and confusion.

"I mean, she doesn't *have* to come to the masjid," Abbas said. "Men do."

Fahim nodded, but his expression was difficult for Abbas to read. "Your wife doesn't come to the masjid?"

Abbas was taken aback by the question, but a moment later he realized his male chauvinism was unwarranted in this case. Fahim was only asking out of genuine curiosity.

"She comes to the masjid," Abbas said. "She'd come every day if she didn't have to work."

Fahim's eyebrows shot up in surprise. "Really? *Maashaa'Allah.* I think the last time my wife came to the masjid was for a *janaazah* about a year ago."

Abbas chuckled. "Well, that's better than a lot of brothers. Some of them don't even bother to come to funerals."

"Unless they knew the person," Fahim said, nodding agreement. "But most of those brothers aren't practicing Muslims."

There was a brief pause as Abbas studied Fahim briefly, unsure if he should ask the question that was on his mind.

"Does your wife practice?"

Fahim appeared a bit uncomfortable with the inquiry, and Abbas wondered if he'd said too much.

A shadow of sadness clouded Fahim's face as he looked beyond Abbas at nothing in particular. Fahim drew in a deep breath and exhaled.

"She prays and fasts," Fahim said tentatively. "But I'm not sure if that counts as practicing Islam."

Abbas creased his forehead, a hint of humored disbelief in his expression. "Of course, it does. In my family, I have dozens of cousins and aunts and uncles who pray only on Eid." He grunted good-naturedly. "And when there's a *janaazah.*"

"But they're not singers and dancers." There was an edge of irritation in Fahim's tone, but Abbas could tell it was in self-rebuke.

"Not professionally," Abbas said tentatively. "But they sing and dance at wedding parties and family gatherings, and many times it's filmed, and the DVD is passed around to friends and family after the event. So, I'm not sure there's much difference."

Fahim's eyebrows shot up. "In front of men?"

Abbas laughed. "Don't look so surprised. Yes, in front of men. But it's not just the women. Everybody joins in."

"And they're Muslim?"

"Yes," he said. "At least most of them are technically."

"Where are you from?"

"My parents are originally from Pakistan. But I was born here."

Fahim looked as if he wanted to ask more but was hesitant.

"Welcome to Desi culture," Abbas said with a grin.

A smile of uncertainty creased one side of Fahim's mouth. "Desi?"

"It's sort of slang for anyone from the countries that were part of the Indian subcontinent before Pakistan, India, and Bangladesh became independent countries."

Fahim nodded, but Abbas could tell that the brother wasn't interested in Desi history.

"Did you convert?" Abbas asked, intentionally changing the subject.

Fahim shook his head. "My parents reverted when I was five years old."

"*Maashaa'Allah*, that's a blessing. So, you grew up Muslim?"

"Yes, *alhamdulillah*," Fahim said, praising God for the blessing.

"I've always admired how strong American converts are." Abbas smiled and shook his head. "You all really do have us beat."

Fahim grunted laughter. "I don't think so. At least not for my family."

"Your parents don't practice?"

"No, I mean, my wife."

Abbas nodded, but he was unsure what to say.

"Maybe our families can get together some time."

Abbas sensed the hopefulness in Fahim's statement, which came out more like an uncertain question intended to test the waters of the strength of the brotherly bond they'd just formed.

"Sure," Abbas said, hoping he sounded more eager than he felt. "That would be nice."

6

"It's not either-or, you know."

Sakinah bit her lower lip as she considered her sister's words. After dropping off Malik and Zaynah at her parents' house, Sakinah had decided to call her sister who lived in Atlanta to get some perspective on her current dilemma. Sakinah loosely gripped the steering wheel, her gaze on the slow-moving traffic on I-495.

"You always say that," Sakinah replied, lifting her right hand to push the earpiece back in place with her index finger. "But sometimes it is."

"I say, to hell with it. You can't please everybody."

"Come on, Kaida. I think I should at least try to keep this family together."

"By moving to Saudi *Arabia*?"

"I don't want to move there, but—"

"Then don't. He's probably got a second wife stashed there anyway. He'll have enough sex to keep him satisfied without you."

Sakinah rolled her eyes. "Kaida, every Muslim man doesn't have a *halaal* mistress. Besides, this has nothing to do with sex. The children need their father, you know."

Kaida's laughter was so loud that Sakinah immediately squeezed her thumb and forefinger together on the wire's volume dial to lower the disruptive sound in her ear.

"You are so stupid, little sister," Kaida said. "So, so stupid. Do you really think that man plans to leave this country without his children? He might leave *you* behind, but not his kids."

Sakinah felt the beginning of a headache. "He wouldn't take them away from me…" But even as she said it, Sakinah couldn't make herself believe it. A sick feeling settled heavily in her gut, telling her that Kaida was right.

"Anyway, you have to have both parents' permission to take children out of the country," Sakinah said with more confidence than she felt.

"And you don't think he's already arranged that?"

"Not without me." Sakinah heard the defiance in her voice, and she wondered why she was so defensive.

"Let me tell you something about Muslim extremists. They fol—"

"Fahim's *not* an extremist."

"—low the laws of the land only when it suits them. Trust, that man will forge a document in a second, notary seal and all, if it means 'making *hijrah* from a *kaafir* land' with his children," Kaida said in cruel mockery of Fahim's religious rhetoric.

Sakinah angrily pursed her lips into a thin line. It was all she could do to keep from responding with an equally cruel comment about Kaida's less-than-upstanding husband. But that would be unfair. Because deep down, Sakinah knew that her sister's words cut so deep not because they were unnecessarily cruel, but because they were a chillingly accurate representation of Fahim. And that was a painful truth that Sakinah herself hadn't yet found it in herself to make peace with.

"Kaida, I have to go."

Kaida's laughter was an unbridled taunt in Sakinah's ear. "Not surprised, little sister. You always conveniently have to go whenever the conversation touches too close to home."

"Kaida, please let's not—"

"You've always been a denier. Hell, you even hide the truth from yourself. That's how you got into that crappy marriage in the first place."

"*As-salaamu'alaikum*," Sakinah hissed through gritted teeth before she silenced the call and yanked the earpiece from her ear.

Sakinah's hands were shaking as she guided the car onto the exit to the upscale Bethesda restaurant where she imagined her business partners were already waiting for her.

Sakinah's phone chimed and vibrated, indicating a message, and Sakinah clenched her jaw. She wished Kaida would just leave well enough alone. But it often felt as if her sister enjoyed making her suffer.

Sakinah slowed to a stop behind a line of cars at a traffic light then lifted her phone before keying in her pin code to read the message.

"where r u, golden child? we're goin 2 order w/o u."

The sides of Sakinah's mouth creased in the beginning of a smile. It was her friend Robyn. Apparently, everyone had arrived except Sakinah.

Glancing between the cell phone screen and the traffic signal, Sakinah quickly typed a reply. *"im close, silver spoon. b patient."*

The light turned green just as the phone chimed and vibrated again as Sakinah set it back down. She immediately lifted it to read Robyn's reply. But she saw Kaida's name instead.

"hope u don't cancel ur visit next weekend. i love u, brat. c ya!"

Sakinah groaned as she put the phone back in place. She immediately regretted considering canceling the three-day trip. As annoying as Kaida was, they were still sisters, and that should count for something.

It should count for everything, in fact.

Because after all was said and done, life boiled down to exactly what people said it did: *Family is everything*. And at that time of emotional turmoil and uncertainty in her marriage, it was at least *Sakinah's* everything.

PART THREE
You Deserve Better

7

Sakinah wondered if Fahim was already home as she walked across the driveway of her parents' home, the late afternoon sun a bright blur behind a cluster of trees in the front yard. A breeze rustled the branches until the leaves swayed. Sakinah tucked her hands into the pockets of her charcoal blazer, but the small pockets exposed her wrists and the bottoms of her palms.

The melancholy was sudden and pronounced, and for a moment Sakinah halted her steps near the front door. A whimper crawled in her throat, and Sakinah's heart raced in bewilderment and self-consciousness at the surge of sadness she was struggling to contain.

"It was March," Sakinah would say years later to a friend, "and I knew that I wouldn't be in America by December. But I didn't know I knew."

At the front door of her parents' home, Sakinah withdrew her hands from her pockets and slid the strap of her designer handbag from her shoulder. She unsnapped the buckle and rummaged through the purse until she heard the familiar jingle and pulled out the ring of keys.

Sakinah inserted the house key into the lock, pushed the front door open, and stepped inside. The faint scent of bleach and peppermint tickled Sakinah's nostrils, and Sakinah blinked back tears as she remembered her mother boiling peppermint leaves and sweetening the tinted liquid with raw honey whenever Sakinah was unwell.

"How was your meeting?"

The sound of her mother's voice prompted Sakinah to look up and find Grace approaching the foyer. Creases formed at the sides of Grace's eyes as she smiled pleasantly and reached behind Sakinah to push the front door closed. Gray peppered the short afro that framed the bronze of Grace's face, and a wide, silk African-style house dress fell regally against Grace's full frame.

A tired smile played at Sakinah's lips. "It was okay."

"Mommy!"

The soft pounding of feet approached until Malik appeared and hugged Sakinah's waist. A faint smell of sweat drifted from Malik's lankly form as he leaned his head against the fabric of Sakinah's business suit. "I won my game!"

Sakinah furrowed her brows as she gently pulled her son away from her to look into his eyes. "Your game?"

"Uncle Jawad took me."

A pang of guilt stabbed Sakinah's chest, but she maintained a pleasant expression. "He did?"

"Oh, Sakinah." Grace locked the door bolt and stepped into the front room, smiling down at her grandson. "That poor child wouldn't stop moping around, so I asked your brother to take him."

Malik smiled wide as his grandmother rubbed his head affectionately. He still wore his bright blue soccer uniform and white kneepads. That morning, Sakinah didn't have the heart to tell her son to change clothes though she knew Fahim would be unable to take Malik like he promised.

"Does Fahim know?" Sakinah released her son and leaned sideways to slip the stilettos off her feet.

A shadow of concern passed over Grace's face as she met her daughter's gaze. "Why?"

Sakinah lifted a shoulder in a shrug as she kneeled down to place her heels on the shoe rack. "I was just wondering."

"*As-salaamu'alaikum*, sis."

43

Sakinah stood as Jawad entered the room. "*Wa'alaikumus-salaam.*" Sakinah's smile was wide as she replied to her younger brother, whose broad shoulders and closely trimmed beard made him appear more mature than her familial opinion would have allowed. She wondered if he'd worn the crisp white and black striped polo shirt and baggy black jeans to the soccer game, or if he'd changed because he had somewhere to go.

"I'm sorry," Jawad said, an awkward smile on his face as he looked at Malik, compassion in his eyes. But the clarity of his tone indicated that he was speaking to his elder sister, not his nephew. "I just remembered how I used to feel when I missed a game."

"I'm glad you took him," Sakinah said sincerely, pinching Malik's cheek playfully then folding her arms in front of her as she gazed proudly at her son. "Otherwise, I would've felt bad myself."

"I made two goals." Malik grinned.

"You did?" Sakinah took his hand and walked into the living room.

"I almost made three."

"He was a sight to see," Jawad said, a tinge of fatherly pride in the lightheartedness of his voice.

Sakinah nodded and rubbed Malik's head playfully. "I'll have to see that myself."

"Michael's Dad recorded it," Malik said.

"Well, then we'll have to ask Michael if we can see it," Sakinah said.

"I think the coach asked him to record it," Jawad said. "So that everyone could probably see it."

Sakinah nodded, her thoughts shifting as she looked at Jawad. "Is Dad home?"

"No," Grace said as she walked toward the kitchen, humor in her tone. "He's out saving the world."

"There's an interfaith conference in California this weekend," Jawad said, smiling as he shook his head at his mother. "Dad and Pastor Williams are speaking."

Sakinah winced at the mention of Daryl's father. "That's good." She forced a smile, but her heart raced and her hands trembled unexpectedly. What was wrong with her?

"Where's Zaynah?" Sakinah asked Jawad after Grace disappeared into the kitchen, Malik trailing behind his grandmother. Sakinah wanted to tell Malik it was time to go home, but she couldn't muster the energy to go back out right then.

"She's sleeping," Jawad said. "At least I think she is."

Sakinah sighed and collapsed into the coach. "Great," she said sarcastically. "Now she won't sleep tonight."

"You know Daryl's a big shot lawyer now." Jawad sat on the couch a comfortable distance from his sister.

"Oh yeah?" Sakinah averted her gaze to her purse that sat primly on her lap, her fingers grasping the handbag to steady her shaking hands. "I heard he was running some workout business for celebrity-wannabes."

Jawad coughed laughter. "You sound bitter."

Sakinah's eyes widened as she glared at her brother. "I do not."

"You do."

"Why would I be bitter about something stupid like that?"

"I was wondering the same thing."

Sakinah groaned and rolled her eyes, but her face was aflame in embarrassment.

"You still sore about what happened?"

Sakinah's heart nearly leaped from her chest. How did Jawad know what happened? Did Daryl track him down and tell him? The mere possibility both terrified and enraged her. *The audacity*—

"Mind your business, little brother," Sakinah snapped.

45

"Sorry," Jawad said, a wounded look on his face. "I didn't know it was a secret. I was only asking because I was thinking about asking him to help me write up a contract with a potential business partner."

"What?" Sakinah narrowed her eyes as she stared at her brother, overcome with confusion.

"You don't think I should?"

"A *business* contract?"

"Yeah…"

Jawad's conflicted expression squeezed Sakinah's heart. A realization came over her right then.

"Oh," Sakinah said weakly, realizing she had misinterpreted her brother's initial comment to be referring to her and Daryl's intimate relationship being abruptly cut off. "Are you hesitating because of that contract Kaida was trying to do with him a few years ago?"

"It's been almost four years, Sakinah," Jawad said, accusation and frustration in his tone. "You can't still be upset about that. He doesn't have to do business with our family if he doesn't want to."

"I couldn't care less whether he does business with the Gordons or not," Sakinah said, unable to mask the defensiveness in her tone. "I forgot about that a long time ago."

And she had.

Until that moment, Sakinah had completely forgotten about the business proposal Kaida had carefully drafted and presented to Daryl Williams, founder and CEO of Get Fit & Hot, in hopes that his company and Songs of the Spirit could work together on some projects.

According to Kaida, when she initially contacted Daryl using her husband's last name and without mentioning Songs of the Spirit specifically, he was interested in the lucrative offer. But as soon as he discovered who Kaida really was and that the business was Sakinah's, he immediately turned down the offer and would not reply to any of Kaida's calls or emails. After that, they remained connected on social media only, but only technically. Though Kaida occasionally liked and commented on some of his posts, he never did the same for hers or even as much as acknowledge any of her comments.

"Then what's your problem?" Jawad said.

Sakinah contorted her face as she glared at Jawad. "Who said there's a problem? I don't care what Daryl does."

Even as she said it, Sakinah could taste the lie on her tongue. She did care, and she hated Daryl for not caring. She hated that he was doing what she herself should have done—cut all ties between them, in life and heart.

"Anyway," Sakinah said, "what makes you think he'll make an exception for you?"

"I'm not asking to do business with him," Jawad said. "I'm paying for legal advice."

Sakinah huffed and rolled her eyes, her dismissiveness intended to convey that she had more insight into Daryl's willingness (or lack thereof) than she actually did.

"I want your opinion on something," Jawad said after a few seconds of awkward silence. His voice was low as he turned to face his sister, his expression guarded and serious.

Sakinah creased her forehead at the sudden shift in energy and tone. "What?"

"Are you free next Saturday?"

"No."

"What about Sunday?"

"Jawad," Sakinah said impatiently with a sigh, "what is this about?"

Jawad was silent for a few seconds as his eyes danced self-consciously in the direction of the kitchen. In that moment, the voices of Grace and Malik talking and laughing together became suddenly audible to Sakinah though she'd heard nothing from them only seconds before.

"I want you to meet somebody."

The smile in Jawad's eyes and the softness in his tone made Sakinah forget her offense of a moment ago. She brought a hand to her mouth in surprise.

"Are you serious?" she whispered, unable to suppress a grin.

"I don't want to say anything until I'm sure."

"Who is she?"

An embarrassed grin creased one side of his mouth. "You'll find out next weekend, *inshaa'Allah*."

Sakinah's smile faded. "But I'm traveling next weekend. Can I meet her the week after? Or maybe late Sunday night?"

Jawad's expression grew concerned. "Are you going to Atlanta again?"

"I have business there," Sakinah said quickly, averting her gaze.

"You know Mom and Dad don't want us talking to Kaida," he whispered in accusation.

"Like I said," Sakinah repeated more firmly, careful to keep her voice low, "I have business there." But even she detected a tremor of dishonesty in her words.

Jawad studied his sister momentarily, as if searching Sakinah's face for the truthfulness of her claim.

"Be careful," he said finally.

Sakinah slapped her thighs as she stood. "I need to get going."

Jawad stood too and grasped Sakinah's arm. "Call me when you get back."

Sakinah turned and scowled at him. "Are you my keeper or something?"

Jawad huffed, releasing her arm. "I'm talking about getting together when you get back."

"Oh, okay," Sakinah said, her face hot in mortification. "I'll let you know."

"Thanks, sis," Jawad said, his tone subdued.

"It's no problem, bro," she said, trying to sound a bit playful. She was hoping to lighten the blow of her previous defensiveness, but her reply came out as a hurried mumble.

She started toward the stairs leading to the guest room on the second level, where she assumed Zaynah was sleeping. "Zay," Sakinah said from the hall, raising her voice. "Zay, baby, we have to go."

Sakinah halted her steps at the wide-open door to the guest room and saw the two queen sized beds neatly made and untouched. She creased her head, wondering where her daughter would be.

Sakinah walked toward her parents' room. "Zay," she said, slightly louder than before. "We have to go."

"Mommy," a groggy voice said, as if coming from a distance.

It took a second for Sakinah to realize that the sound was coming from the loft that her mother used as an office. Sakinah fought a feeling of irritation as she walked up another flight of steps. When Sakinah was growing up, no one was allowed in the loft. Not even Hakim went there, though Sakinah imagined that her father merely found no need to, while Sakinah and her sister and brother had been expressly forbidden from entering. The loft was "Grace's domain" as their mother affectionately called it, and if anyone "trespassed" they were swiftly punished. There was no lock or door obstructing entry into the loft, but there might as well have been.

As a child, Sakinah treasured the moments when her mother sent her there on a quick errand to fetch a book, notepad, or file folder that she needed. During those rare moments, Sakinah would saunter and drink in the organized disarray of the room—the wide desk scattered with papers next to a computer that had been changed to newer models over the years, the file cabinet just an arm's reach away from the leather swivel office chair, and shelves of books stretching the length of an entire wall.

Opposite the wall shelving the library of books was a futon with an array of pillows covering it. This had been Sakinah's favorite part of the room. There were moments that Sakinah would cautiously sit on it, enjoying the comfort of the pillows as she turned her body awkwardly to stare at the framed pictures and newspaper clippings hanging on the wall above the futon. Grace's Hall of Fame. That's what her mother called it.

Sakinah learned more about her mother's life during those stolen moments staring at that wall than she did talking to Grace herself. There was an aged photo of Grace as a teen wearing black leotards and proudly holding a trophy, surrounded by other young women dressed similarly. There was an aged photo of Grace dressed in a shimmery violet gown adorned by a corsage. There was a newspaper clipping of Grace holding a large framed certificate, flanked by two important-looking men.

But it was the center frame that always held Sakinah's attention most. It was the only frame that did not feature Grace herself. It was a clipped newspaper article about Hakim Gordon dated a few years before Sakinah was born. *"Community activist delivers moving eulogy at the funeral of friend and fellow activist, Daryl Williams,"* the caption said. Above the caption was a photo of Hakim with his arm around Daryl, both men laughing at something.

"I was named after him," Daryl had told Sakinah one day when they were still in high school, a trace of sadness in his tone. It was the second time he'd said this to her, but apparently, he had forgotten that when they'd first met as

children, he'd eagerly and proudly shared with her the inspiration behind his name. Sakinah herself sometimes forgot that detail from that day, because the Williams family had been so insignificant to her at the time.

But as a teenager, Sakinah had already figured as much, given their identical names and the late Daryl being young Daryl's uncle, Pastor Williams's brother. *"I have the same newspaper clipping,"* he'd said after Sakinah revealed to him the details of the clip hanging on her mother's private wall. *"But I can't bring myself to hang it on any wall."* When Sakinah asked why, Daryl had said, *"Because what that article doesn't say is that my uncle took his own life."* He grunted. *"I'm not sure that's a legacy I want to uphold."*

Presently, Sakinah entered the loft and found Zaynah pushing herself into a sitting position from where she lay on the futon.

"Nana said I can help her work," Zaynah said, a tinge of defensiveness in her groggy voice. It was at that moment that Sakinah realized that she was grimacing at her daughter.

"Get your things," Sakinah said brusquely, surprised by the irritation in her tone. "We have to go."

Sakinah's eyes rested briefly on the framed newspaper photo of her father and Daryl's namesake. *"It's a reminder of why I married your father,"* Grace had said years ago, her eyes lingering affectionately on the clipping as Sakinah handed her mother the cup of tea she'd requested brought up to the loft. Moments before her mother's reflection, Sakinah had gotten up the nerve to ask Grace why it was the only framed photo or clipping that wasn't about her mother herself. *"It puts my life into focus and reminds me that everything I gave up to be a wife and mother was worth it in the end."*

8

"Hold on a second." Fahim covered the mouthpiece to the house phone as he pulled the receiver away from his ear. He heard the front door open and close, and annoyance gripped his chest.

"Daddy!" Malik's excited voice was far away, but his hurried footsteps drew closer.

"Thanks for getting back with me," Fahim said as he put the phone back to his ear. "I'll send the paperwork right away *inshaa'Allah*...No problem. I understand...Of course...*Wa'alaikumussalaam.*"

Fahim returned the receiver to the base just as the bedroom door banged open and Malik rushed to Fahim's side, breathless in excitement.

"I won my game!"

Fahim stood and reached under Malik's outstretched arms before lifting him proudly in the air. "You did, huh?"

"Mm hm," Malik nodded, grinning. "And I made two goals."

Fahim set Malik down and balled up his right hand. Malik followed suit, and they playfully punched each other's fist.

"That's my boy," Fahim said.

Satisfied and still grinning to himself, Malik rushed out of the room, forgetting to close the door behind him. Fahim was still smiling when Sakinah appeared in the doorway, her arms crossed. Fahim's eyes traced the form-fitting blazer and pants that his wife wore. He frowned and turned his back as he opened a drawer and pretended to search for something.

"*As-salaamu'alaikum*, Daddy."

The sound of Zaynah's voice prompted Fahim to halt his search and turn around, one hand still in the drawer. Fahim hadn't seen his daughter standing behind Sakinah. Or maybe Zaynah just arrived.

"*Wa'alaiku-mus-salaam*, sweetie."

"Can I be in the ballet competition? Mommy said to ask you."

Fahim cut his eyes in Sakinah's direction and managed to glower at his wife imperceptibly, but Sakinah's blasé expression was difficult to read as she met his gaze unblinking. His irritation was tempered only by Zaynah's large, innocent eyes eager for her father's approval. Her kinky curls were pulled back into a single ponytail, red marbles against the top of her head and at the end of the fraying braid at the back of her neck. Fahim's lips shut firmly into a thin line as he fought the urge to smile at his daughter affectionately.

"Zaynah, did you pray Maghrib?" Fahim finally managed to utter. He didn't want to ask his daughter outright to leave, but he would if he had to. He was furious at Sakinah and was bursting at the seams to let his wife know exactly how he felt.

Zaynah's face twisted in dissatisfaction, and she pouted as she left the room.

"And close the door," Fahim said, raising his voice authoritatively. Gone was any inclination to sympathize with his daughter.

Fahim watched as Sakinah's eyes followed their daughter out the door, which Zaynah did not close. Anger rose in his chest as he watched his wife walk casually over to the bed and set her handbag on the nightstand. "I have to pray mysel—"

"What the hell were you thinking?" Fahim's chest was almost touching the back of Sakinah. He had to resist yanking the collar of her fancy business suit.

Sakinah snapped her head in Fahim's direction, her eyes wide in shock. "What are you talking about?"

"You know what I'm talking about."

"No, I don't." Sakinah wedged her way past Fahim and headed toward their master bathroom, her expression a mixture of confusion and disgust.

"Listen to me when I'm talking to you."

Sakinah halted her steps and slowly turned her body toward Fahim.

Fahim huffed his impatience. Was this what he had to resort to in order to get his wife's attention?

"I-am-not-your-child." Sakinah's tone was measured, and she spoke through gritted teeth.

Fahim walked up to Sakinah and leaned his face toward her. He pushed his forefinger into the fabric of her blouse over her chest. "But you *are* my wife. Act like it."

Sakinah unbuttoned her suit jacket and shrugged it off then folded it over the wrinkled white fabric at the crease in her elbow.

"I've been trying." Sakinah met Fahim's gaze coldly as she leaned her face toward him.

The attractive smoothness of Sakinah's face, the baby hairs peeking out at the edges of the black fabric tied on her head, and the sweet scent of perfume made Fahim weak in desire. But he refused to soften his taut expression.

"But I don't want the job anymore," she said.

Sakinah was already in the bathroom and had shut the door when Fahim registered the meaning of her words. The sound of water running taunted him, and he was at the door in a matter of seconds. He twisted the door handle and found that it was locked.

"What the—" he said under his breath. He pounded on the door with the flat of his hand, the noise deafening.

"Open the door, Sakinah."

The running water stopped, but there was only silence.

He wrestled the door handle and shook it until it loosened. "Open the *door*."

The door opened as he raised his fist to pound on the wood again. Sakinah's face glistened with water as she held the door handle, wrinkling her nose at him as if seeing him for the first time and being sorely disappointed. She turned her body sideways to walk past him, and her silence enraged him.

"Sakinah." Fahim spoke in a more controlled voice.

"*Allahu'akbar*." Sakinah faced a corner of the room as she raised her hands as if in surrender, signaling the start of prayer.

Fahim had to fight the urge to disrupt her worship. It was beyond disrespectful for her to use Salaah, of all things, to ignore him.

Fahim paced the floor of their room as he waited impatiently for Sakinah to finish praying. His chest tightened in frustration when she remained in prostration longer than usual, her face touching the ground peacefully while he could barely keep still.

"Are you okay?"

Fahim started at the sound of his son's voice. He turned to see Malik, still dressed in his soccer uniform, standing at the room door, a worried expression on his young face.

"Yes, Malik. Go take a shower."

"I heard a loud noise."

"Everything's okay. Now, *leave*." Malik turned and rushed down the hall as Fahim walked quickly toward the room door and slammed it shut.

When Fahim turned back around, he saw Sakinah sitting and turning her head to the right then to the left, signaling the end of prayer.

"You shouldn't ignore me like that," Fahim said.

Sakinah relaxed her legs and folded them in front of her as she continued to murmur prayers, still facing the corner of the room. She didn't acknowledge her husband's presence or his words. She moved her thumb up and down the spaces on her fingers, enumerating the praises of Allah in *dhikr*.

"You can cut it out now," Fahim said, growing agitated. "Prayer is over. You need to pay attention to me now."

Sakinah drew in a deep breath and sighed as she looked toward the ceiling. For a moment, Fahim thought he had his wife's attention. But she continued murmuring the *dhikr* that was customary after formal prayers.

A tinge of guilt stung Fahim's conscience. He should let his wife finish her *dhikr*. It wasn't right for him to demand that she turn her attention away from her Creator just to listen to him. But he had that right, Fahim reasoned. A husband had to be obeyed, he'd learned in one of the imam's classes—even if the wife was engaged in worship. Only obligatory prayers were the exception. And *dhikr* didn't fall in that category.

Fahim opened his mouth to say something, but Sakinah, still sitting, turned around before he could.

"I want a divorce," she said.

Sakinah's words were calm and deliberate, but Fahim stepped back as if wounded, doubting he'd heard her correctly. The words sapped the last reserves of the aggravation from him. He felt weak all of a sudden.

"I want a divorce." She raised her voice this time, as if to remove any doubts as to the meaning of her words. "You're overbearing and cruel, and I hate living with you."

Fahim was offended by her words, but the trembling of his wife's lower jaw and the tears shining in her eyes squeezed a soft spot in his chest. Panic gripped him and he walked over to the bed on weakened legs, struggling to catch his breath. But he did his best to hide it. If there was any moment that he needed to show absolutely no trace of weakness, it was now.

"What?" He'd intended his tone to sound firm with rebuke, but his voice was barely above a whisper as his body met the mattress of their bed when he sat down.

"I never wanted to marry you," she said.

Fahim was stunned into silence, feeling as if he'd been punched in the gut.

Sakinah's eyes pooled with tears, but Sakinah wiped them away with the bottom of her palms before they spilled down her cheeks. "But I agreed because I thought you were a good Muslim. I thought marrying you would make me a better Muslim." Her last words came out as a whimper, and she sniffed, wiping her eyes once again.

"But you're just a sexist hypocrite," she continued, her words verging on a whine. "And I hate you. I hate everything about you. I don't care if I'm not a good wife. I don't care if I'm not a good Muslim. I don't even care if I'm a good person."

She looked away from him now, and tears slipped down her cheeks in disjointed paths. "Divorce me," she said. "At least then I can be free of you. At least I'll have that. Oh, may Allah free me of you." She sucked in her breath audibly and moaned in agony. "May He remove your face from me. May He remove you from my life. May He give me someone better. A man, *any* man, so long as he's a real man. And not you."

Fahim's heart fell at her last words, and he was numb in trepidation and humiliation. He felt lightheaded all of a sudden. But even then, a surge of anger burrowed its way through his chest. *How dare she. The nerve—*

"And may Allah give you someone better than me," Sakinah said finally, dropping her chin to her chest as if suddenly ashamed of herself. Her last words were a high-pitched moan. "You deserve it."

Who Am I?

The four-part read-aloud story that became a stage play and inspired the young adult novel, *The Friendship Promise*

PART ONE
I'll Be Honest...

1

Have you ever asked the question, "Who am I?" or "What am I doing?" or Where am I going?" Yeah, yeah, yeah, I know they're boring questions. And typical. The kind of questions your mother or father are always asking you to *ponder*. And hey, I'll be honest, I didn't think about 'em much years ago.

And I still don't.

But I'll be honest again. I think about 'em more than I used to. Sometimes when I get to thinking, I say to myself, "Girl, do you really know who you are?" But I sometimes shrug it off. And I honestly feel stupid. Because, who sits and thinks about stuff like "Who am I?" It's just corny. Not cool. I mean, huh, what am I supposed to tell my best friend if she calls and says, "What's up? Whatcha doing?" What am I supposed to say, "Yeah, nothing much, just trying to figure out who am I"?

But I realized it's not such a bad question after all. And I guess you can say I learned that the old fashioned way. Through experience. Or, actually through my best friend. We don't see each other much anymore. Actually, not at all. But hopefully one day we'll be back in touch.

But, anyway, I gotta tell you about her. She was my girl. I mean, we were *tight*. (Laughs). We spent so much time together her parents would joke about adopting me! And I'm sure my parents felt the same about her.

I met her when we were in, what? Seventh grade...I think. Yeah, seventh grade, because our parents introduced us to each other, because, you know, they were good friends and they wanted their children to get to know each other, and I'm sure they saw us getting older, starting to look more like women and decided it was time for us to have friends. Muslim friends. Because you know how this world is. Crazy. At least that's what my parents always say. So they wanted me to be around some "good people."

But anyway, we didn't care too much for each other at first. You know how it is. The people your parents want you to be around are not always cool. Not your people. You know.

And I know it's not good, but at that time—as a seventh grader who went to public school since kindergarten—I didn't care too much for Muslims. I know it's a horrible thing now that I think about it, but you gotta understand, I was caught up in all the stuff that, well, *you* probably like now. Clothes, shopping, and (smirks) looking good. (Yes, I admit, although I wore my *khimaar*, I snuck in my mom's makeup cabinet sometimes and dressed my face up a bit).

But anyway, back to my best friend. We hated each other at first, so whenever she came over, I pretended to be bored, and she did too. Or maybe she wasn't pretending, but I was. At least I think I was. It's hard to say now, but anyway, I wanted friends. I mean, who doesn't? But I just didn't like my parents pushing somebody on me.

2

I don't know how long we managed to appear disinterested in each other, but it faded eventually. Of course. And I don't even remember exactly how and when, but we started to talk. And, gosh, now that I look back, I really liked her from the beginning. In many ways, she was who I wanted to be. She was really smart, and really pretty, but I would've never told her. And as many years as we've been friends, I've never actually admitted it to her, but I sure did wish I was her sometimes.

But anyway, around the time we started seventh grade, we started wearing *hijaab* and have been wearing it since then. At least I have. But Samira, oh yeah that's her name, but Samira would take it off sometimes. Not in front of her parents though. She would sneak and do it. And although I wasn't exactly what I would've considered religious, I would tell her not to do it, at least sometimes I would. I don't know what I thought about *hijaab* then, but I know one thing, I never had the nerve to take it off. It just didn't seem right. But Samira had the nerve. (Laughs) Like she had the nerve to do a lot of things. But don't get me wrong, there was no mistaken Samira, she was Muslim. And proud. But like most others, and like me too, she was weak in some areas. But we always prayed. I don't know, but for some reason that hadeeth scared the mess out of us, you know, the one that said the difference between us and them is the *salaah* and whoever leaves it falls into *kufr*. So no matter what crazy stuff we did, we always prayed. (Laughs) I don't know how much concentration we had or if any of 'em were accepted, b/c much of the time it was just going thru the motions with our minds elsewhere. But we said 'em. Even if on our bad days we were making 'em all up before bed. But we said 'em though.

Gradually, we started doing everything together. And we ended up even camping out on each other's bedroom floor whenever we got a chance. And believe me, we'd make up any excuse to have a sleepover. We'd have an I'm-bored-sleepover, a please-can-just-go-sleepover, an it's-not-fair-if-I-can't-sleepover, or even a cram-sleepover, which basically is just a fun study session the night before a test. And oh yes, by eighth grade we had vowed to take all the same classes. (Laughs) We had even decided to major in the same thing in college! (Laughs again). And we never did decide what that major would be.

3

But anyway, by time we hit high school we were inseparable, and needless to say, our parents were pleased. Their plan had worked. Their two Muslim daughters were best friends after all. But don't get me wrong, that didn't mean they let us do whatever. They still kept a close watch on us, and over time they noticed things about us and treated us accordingly.

For example, with Samira, although I'm not sure if they ever found out about her taking off her *khimaar* at school sometimes (or at the mall), they did suspect she was the weaker Muslim in the relationship. And so a lot of things were usually done at my house if her parents weren't able to supervise. I suppose they just saw in Samira that love for the world, you know, TV, movies, and yes, even music. I didn't dare...at least not unless Samira convinced me to just watch, look, or listen. And I admit it, I did watch some crazy movies and listen to a little music, but I didn't have half the nerve of Samira, who would buy the stuff! I have no idea how she pulled *that* off, but she did.

I guess I already mentioned that Samira was smart. But that's an understatement. She was an absolute brain. Yeah, we both got good grades, straight *A*s mostly, but I had to work so hard to do it, but for her it was a breeze.

Samira was a pretty self motivated person and did what she wanted and often things went the way she wanted, when she wanted. She stood her own, so to speak, even with her parents, and I admired that then. But I'm not so sure now if that's the best trait for a person to have with her parents. But anyway, Samira did usually get her way with her parents, and if they did not give it to her, she would argue with them for hours to convince them of how unfair it was or how badly she needed, or wanted, whatever it was.

And it usually worked.

Usually.

PART TWO
No Internet! No Chat Rooms!

4

But one thing her parents would not give in to was her desire to have internet in the house.

"But all the kids have it," she would complain sometimes. "It's not fair!" she would protest at others. "You're so extreme!" she would blow up at times.

But still. Her parents were not changing their position. They didn't want internet in their house, and that was final.

But Samira never let them hear the end of it.

And she never let me hear the end of it.

"Gosh, I wish my parents weren't so darn extreme," she would always complain to me.

And I admit, I indulged her. "Your parents are whack," I would agree.

Believe it or not, it was one of our deepest bonding experiences, because it was one thing we could always agree on. Her parents were overprotective and extreme.

At least that's what I thought at the time.

And although I never said it, and although I didn't quite realize it myself, probably b/c I would never've wanted to admit it, but part of me understood why her parents wouldn't give her internet. I'm not saying I supported it or anything, but I guess with a little bit of 20/20 hindsight, I can see why, you know.

There was just something about Samira that just grabbed your attention when you saw her. She had that twinkle in her eye, not like a happy twinkle, but an up-to-something twinkle. And you knew that whenever she came around, something fun was going to happen. No, not the kinda fun parents would like, but fun nonetheless. 'Cause she always had something up her sleeve. And as for me, I was always excited to see what. But I'm sure her parents' excitement was when I or anyone else *didn't* see what.

So I'm sure you can see how the internet could be a sticky issue with someone like Samira. But like I said, I know I would never've admitted it at the time.

But as I told you before, there was no stopping Samira, or at least that's how she (and I) saw it. So what did Samira do?

She just used my internet.

I wasn't supposed to let her. Or I should say my parents weren't supposed to let her, and they told me, no internet, whenever she came over. Yeah, I know my parents weren't totally into that rule, but I'll tell you one thing, when it came to other parents' rules, my parents abiding completely. It's like that little parent pact they all have, you know, kinda like "I got your back even if I don't understand why I do."

So my parents forbade internet use while she was over, and I obeyed. At least that was my intention.

But (sucks teeth) Samira, she was hard to turn down. 'Cause although she had that 'evil twin' side so to speak, she still had that heart warming side too, that would convince you that, even when she was wrong, she was in fact the victim.

"'C'mon Anisa," she'd say in that whiny voice of her. "Just for a second. It'll be real quick. I just wanna look something up."

"But Samira," I would remind her gently, more out of knowing I should than any sincerity on my part, "you know what your parents said."

She'd just suck her teeth and wave her hand and say, "Yeah, but you know they're just being extreme. I mean, Gosh, the whole worlds on line, and I'm still living in the Dark Ages. I don't know why my parents won't just make us cook dinner on stones."

I would giggle. "But still," I would manage to say with a straight face. "You know it's not right."

She would roll her eyes. "God knows I heard that already." And I knew she was referring to her parents. "Is anything *right* in this world?"

I would just get quiet whenever she asked that, because I knew where that conversation was headed, and to be honest I was afraid to go there. I knew that if I did I might end up thinking the same way, you know, about the world, and Islam, and Muslims. But I just wouldn't, no—I just couldn't. It was way too scary to imagine that—.

"Just for a few minutes," she would say quickly with that innocent grin of hers.

I would laugh uncomfortably, but I'd hope Samira didn't see my discomfort. "But my parents'll kill me!"

"Oh let 'em," she'd joke with that grin of hers, promptly situating herself in front of my PC at that same time. "I promise I'll come to the funeral."

I would laugh, of course. Who wouldn't? She was hilarious sometimes.

And meanwhile, she was already logging onto the internet. (We had one of those log in screens where the password was already there when you logged on).

And predictably, I didn't stop her. And for a second, I thought, what the heck. No one would know. We had a separate line for internet, so it wasn't like my parents could pick up the phone or anything.

But they could walk in the room anytime.

At that moment, after she'd logged on, Samira would turn to give me a look and say, "What are you just standing there for? Go lock the door."

And chuckling uncomfortably, like a robot, I'd go lock the door. And on the internet she was surfing pages and pages of I don't know what. I was too overwhelmed with guilt to even look. My mind would be wandering to my parents. What were they doing? Would they find out? What would they do to me? Oh, and what about Samira's parents? They would never trust me anymore. They'd think I wasn't trustworthy. Were they right?

Most times I'd grab a book and read mindlessly on my bed, hoping and hoping she'd get off soon. I didn't know what I'd do if my parents found out. I'd be utterly speechless. I was sure they'd never understand. And gosh, I didn't even understand it myself. What was I *doing*?

But for reassurance, I would glance up ever so often to ascertain she was going to "innocent" sites. And thank God, she was. Or at least innocent, considering. She'd go to fashion magazine sites or sites about the latest singers or bands or rap groups. Whatever was in.

But, I don't know why, but I never expected her to go anywhere else. But of course she did. And her first venture was to chat rooms.

And as much as I surfed the internet, I'd never, ever gone to chat rooms before. They were completely off limits. Yeah, I'd go to message boards. Islamic message boards, but not chat rooms. Not even "Islamic ones."

It was just…unacceptable. And I wouldn't dare.

But I should've known Samira *would* dare.

I didn't really find out until she began talking to the screen. And that wasn't all that unusual, b/c she'd do that every now and then. We all do, I suppose. But it was the *way* she was talking to the screen that made me suspicious.

"Yeah, idiot, I'm a sister!" she shout out suddenly in one of her conversations with the screen. "Look at my screen name!"

Of course, this perked my ears, and I grew curious. Real curious.

I'd be sitting there watching her long hair move and bounce as she'd do hand gestures and head motions toward the screen that glowed around her head. "Can-you-read?" she'd say the words slowly as if typing them with her voice. "I-am-a-sister!"

At that point, I'd be in both denial and self-protection, denial b/c I didn't want to believe she was actually in a chat room and self-protection b/c I didn't want my parents to hear. So I'd sit there, speechless, wondering, what should I do?

"What are you doing?" I finally asked casually, playing it cool.

She'd wave her hand at me or hold up her finger to let me know she was in the middle of something. Then she'd burst out laughing, giggling mischievously as she typed something. "You won't believe this guy!" she'd shout at me, as if I was in on this chat room thing too. And the word "guy" would stick out painfully in my ear. She was in a chat room talking to a *guy*? This was too much. "He thinks it's like a symbol of corruption for a sister not to cover!"

I swallowed. "Really?" I asked, as if amused, surprising myself by the interest in my own voice.

"Yeah!" she'd laugh. "He's nuts."

I mentally convinced myself it was okay. She was talking to Muslims, at least. And it was an Islamic discussion. But when my eyes grazed the screen, I saw him asking where she lived. And to my surprise she told him. And then she asked him the same!

I couldn't take it. I had to look away. I turned and re-immersed myself into reading my book. I had to do something to keep busy. Although I'm not sure my brain caught any of the words that my eyes passed over.

I'm not sure how I lasted through those days. And Lord knows there were many of them. I'm not sure I ever got comfortable. But I somehow became used to it. What should I care if Samira talked to brothers online? I never actually *approved*, I'd convince myself. She'd let *herself* do it. I never said she *could*.

But should I say something to her? That's the question that absolutely killed me. Shouldn't I say something like, don't do that, or it's not right?

Somewhere in the far back of my mind, I suppose, I knew that, yes, I should tell here that. But I just couldn't.

Or maybe, no, it was for sure. I just *wouldn't*.

I don't know how long I let this go on. And in my own room! I was so horrible, I knew, and I'd even watch the chat sometimes. And, I admit, some of the discussions were interesting. Although I know my parents would never approve of sisters and brothers in private chat rooms discussing issues with no supervision. And now that I think about it, I'm not even sure if the other Muslims in the chat room had any business there either.

Either way. They were there, and I was there…I suppose…if you think about it like that. I'd even catch myself laughing at some of the conversation and telling Samira what to say to someone, even a brother, if they made a dumb point. And when I think back, I don't even know how I got to that point. But, God knows I started to enjoy it and look forward to those chats.

Until the day Samira went to another chat room.

PART THREE

Isn't He Cute?

5

Or maybe Samira had gone to another chat room long before that and I just never knew.

In fact, now that I think back, she had to have gone long before that.

But anyway, I just happened to find out one day when my eye happened to catch this picture of this guy on the screen.

For a moment, I thought it was one of those advertisements, you know, pop up ads—like "Lose 20 lbs. In a week!" type ads. But when it stayed up a bit longer than I thought it should, I just got this weird feeling.

"Who's that?" I heard myself ask before realizing it.

"Come look!" Samira giggled, no shame traceable in her voice.

And like a zombie in obedience, I came—hoping, *praying* that she'd just surfed the web and found somebody's personal website by accident.

"Isn't he cute?" she squealed.

As shocking as the words were to my ears (we never discussed boys before!), I giggled. I actually giggled! And I barely recognized my own laugh, mentally stunned that I found any humor in this. "Yeah," I heard myself say further, stiffening at the reality of what I'd just said. Weren't we supposed to be lowering our gazes or something! I mean, a brother in swimming trunks is hardly Islamic garb!

And I'd never even said a brother was even half-way good looking, let alone "cute." And I'd sat here and actually confirmed that one was! And was staring at him nodding approvingly! What was I doing!

"Is this the brother you were arguing with in the chat room?" I asked, approval still in my voice, and still awkward to my ears.

She shot me a confused glanced, rolled her eyes, and waved her hand. "No, *this*" she corrected, her tone suggesting this brother was much more important, a grin forming on her face as she did a quick approving nod, "is Jason."

The name stung my ears, and I felt my whole head become hot.

Jason wasn't a Muslim name. At least not where I'm from.

Maybe he converted?

I don't know how I managed to, but I asked slowly, cautiously, "Is he Muslim?"

She sucked her teeth and rolled her eyes again. "Of course not."

I was floored. And it was a sheer miracle that I hadn't fainted. "Wh-wh-who's Jason?" I asked, petrified. There was no concealing my shock now—even if I wanted to.

Frustrated with me, she closed the picture by clicking on the little X with the mouse.

And I know she didn't intent me to, but right under that picture, I saw an e-mail! An e-mail! How on earth did Samira have e-mail!

O Lord! She opened up one of those free accounts right under my nose. And I didn't even have a clue!

And who was this Jason?

I don't know how I got thru that day—or the next—or the next or the next. B/c every day after that, Samira was on the computer with this Jason person. And I didn't bother asking *what* they were talking about, b/c I could hardly swallow the fact *that* they were talking! I mean, there was a man—a 20-year-old man on the other end of that computer! That was just too much for my mind to handle.

After that, she'd sometimes tell me about the conversations with him on the net and how he was from Florida (thank God, I'd think, at least he was hundreds of miles away). I guess that made me feel better. A safe distance I suppose. Not actually the best scenario, but I counted it as a blessing.

And I must've held onto that "blessing" for about a week, b/c it was about a week later that Samira came over my house with a grin spread across that pretty face of hers. She invited herself into my room, closed the door behind her, and locked it. I just knew she was heading for the computer, but, instead, she plopped on the carpet in the middle of my floor.

She didn't have to beckon me. I knew. It was heart-to-heart time.

I loved heart-to-heart. It was a time for us to share secrets and just be friends. It was one of my fondest memories with Samira, those heart-to-heart talks.

So glad to be having one of our talks, and especially relieved that she was not getting on the computer (at least not just yet), I happily sat in the middle of the floor and sat in "Friendship Style"

Wait (laughs), I gotta explain this friendship style thing. And yeah, yeah, I know it's kinda silly, and even now it makes me giggle.

Friendship Style meant we sat knee to knee, holding hands, with our heads leaning toward each other, sometimes touching, and before we start we'd recite in our "friendship" whisper, "Friends forever, friends forever, friends for ever more."

I think we did it as a joke at first, and I suppose we were both too shy to say we actually liked it, so we just kept on doing it until it became "Friendship Style"

But anyway, after assuming our sitting position and recited our usual words, she said quickly, "You first."

"No," I told her honestly, "I don't have anything to say."

"Okay," she said so quickly and so happily that I knew here initial invitation for me to talk was just out of politeness. "But let's recite it again."

She had never before asked us to recite it twice. But I shrugged and in between giggles, we recited, "Friends forever, friends forever, friends for ever more."

A second later the room grew quiet, and although she was still smiling, her face grew serious and of course I grew curious. And I was wild with excitement for whatever Samira would tell me. Samira's heart-to-hearts were always good, and at times, I wished I had such an interesting life as hers.

"You promise not to break the friendship promise?" she asked for reassurance.

And she'd never done that before either.

"Yes," I promised her hurriedly, anxious to hear her heart-to-heart.

"Okay," she grinned wildly, then she said quickly, "I'm gonna meet him."

For a moment the reality of her words escaped my ears— or perhaps it was that they escaped my senses. So it took me a second or two to realize who this "him" was.

And as it hit me, Samira was grinning so hugely and was so elated that I'm quite sure she didn't realize my shocked expression. She just kept on chatting and grinning and giggling and chatting and grinning and giggling. And I listened mindlessly.

I heard her voice but I don't recall the words.

The only words that stood out were "mall," and "he's coming here."

"Wh-wh-when?" I stuttered.

"Tomorrow!" she announced proudly. She was so excited that I almost felt guilty for being a bad sport. But then again, could one really be a good sport about this?

But she didn't seem to notice my reservations.

Thank God.

Apparently, she'd tuned me out much like I'd tuned her out. But one thing did catch my ear, and that was when she mentioned me.

"So you're just going to act normal and say we're going to the mall," she concluded. And I'd missed it. I had no idea how she managed to work *me* into all of this.

Lord knows I wanted no part of it!

Cautiously, I asked her to again go over what I was supposed to do. I tried my best to sound like I wanted to know for clarification and not b/c I wasn't listening.

In any case, she didn't seem to have noticed. And she just simply repeated the plan.

And this time, I understood.

O Lord! I understood.

We were going to go to the mall, where she'd meet him, while I wandered from store to store, for about an hour, when we'd meet back in front of Sears, where her parents would pick us up and we'd go home. And then it would be all over.

O Lord, if it could've only been over right then!

"Wh-wh-when?" I stuttered. Perhaps, I'd already asked that, but I'd lost my train of thought momentarily.

"Tomorrow," she repeated, slight frustration traceable in her voice. I guess that was the first hint she received that I wasn't really listening. But still, she was in her own world, practically oblivious to my presence.

To make a long story short, and Lord knows it's a long story, and I still groan at the thought. But I agreed.

PART FOUR
The Mall Meet-up

6

So, Lord only knows how, but I ended up at the local mall at noon the next day—and I remember, it was a Saturday (the only day we were ever allowed to go to the mall during the school year). And not knowing what on earth I was doing, five minutes after her parents dropped us off, I was wandering from store-to-store. Alone.

I was only half-there at the mall that day. Most days I'd have noticed the stares b/c of my khimaar, but not that day. My heart was pounding so violently that I momentarily thought I was having a heart attack. I had no idea where Samira was meeting this Jason person, but it gave me chills to think that he was actually here, I mean really *here*, somewhere in the mall.

And I don't think I could've stomached the thought of Samira being with him.

But I kept my cool—or perhaps, I should say, I appeared to have kept my cool. And I somehow made it thru that tormenting hour. I dutifully showed up in Sears, as scheduled, to meet Samira.

In an effort to get some fresh air, I sat on a bench outside the store, near where people were waiting for the bus. It just seemed like inside I couldn't breathe. Gosh, I kept thinking, did I have asthma or something?

Fifteen minutes passed, and I started getting antsy. Where was Samira? Her parents would be here any minute, and what would I tell them when they didn't see Samira with me? I'd have to have *some* explanation as to why we weren't together. And O Lord! I just remembered at that moment, I even had Samira's khimaar in my purse! She was going to get it back when we met. Or at least that was the plan.

When twenty minutes had passed, I became almost frantic and struggled to calm myself. I wanted to make du'aa to Allah to help me and get Samira here before her parents. But, I mean, I just didn't feel right asking for help from Allah in doing wrong. And yeah, at that moment, I knew, no matter how much I'd mentally dodged it before. We were doing wrong. There was no other way to describe it. O Lord I knew I'd never do *this* again.

So I sat there—in utter panic—drenched in sin, and more terrified of the prospect of my parents knowing than the knowledge that Allah knew all along.

What would I say to them if they found out? *O Allah! They trusted me! Please, please, get me out of this, just this one, and I swear I'd never do it again!*

When thirty minutes passed, I got up and paced, and paced, and paced and paced. I guess my panic must've been obvious, b/c some woman asked me if I was okay. I told her that I was fine, and she walked off, unsure, but telling me to take care anyway.

Where was Samira?!! I was sick with fear and worry! *C'mon Samira, c'mon Samira, C'mon!!! Your parents'll be here any second!!!* My thoughts screamed.

And like a bomb exploding all of a sudden, the blue Camry pulled in front of the mall and stopped right where I was sitting. Momentarily, I shut my eyes. This wasn't Samira's car I told myself. This couple wasn't her parents. It couldn't be!

But when they beeped, I looked up and saw her mother's khimaar. My heart sank.

Why hadn't I waited *inside* the mall? Was I crazy? At least inside I could've lingered and stalled a bit, and had her parents wait. At least until I found her.

But O Lord! I was standing there, probably going pale. And meanwhile, no Samira in sight! And O Allah! I had her khimaar in my purse! So even if she did show up, there'd be disaster!

I was absolutely going to lose it. I didn't know *what* to do.

And I guess it must've shown on my face b/c a second later Samira's mother emerged from the car, and her concerned expression was unmistakable.

Lord knows I don't know what I said to her exactly, but at some point I broke down. Yeah, I mean really broke down. The tears came and all I remember is shortly after that they went searching for her. I don't know if they asked me to, but I was too shocked to look for her. I guess part of me was hoping she'd come around the corner and that I should just wait there like we planned, you know, just in case she came to meet me as scheduled.

Everything happened so fast after that. They say time flies when you're having fun, but believe you me, I wasn't having fun. And I'm not even sure if I'd say time flew, but it sure did seem to just stop. I mean everything, and before I knew it, it was pitch black outside, the mall was closed, and the only people there were me, Samira's parents, and two police officers asking us questions.

They couldn't find her. I was stunned. All this time, and they couldn't find her.

She wasn't there, they told us, but I insisted she was. She wasn't there, they had to tell me over and over again. They'd searched the whole place and no one was there. They'd even had other officers check all the utility rooms and bathrooms and they checked all the hidden camera footage. And nothing. Absolutely nothing.

So. She wasn't there.

They kept asking me if she had run away, but I kept saying she didn't. And then I told them the truth. Every bit of it. Yes, I broke the friendship promise.

But what choice did I have?

Samira would kill me I thought.

And so would my parents.

O Lord! My parents.

They were on their way. So far, all they knew was that Samira was missing. And I was petrified to have them find out that I had anything to do with this crazy plan.

But they did find out, shortly after they arrived, and I couldn't look at them as the officers talked to them. I just buried my head in my hands and cried and cried and cried and cried.

I suppose I went into depression after that. I barely ate. I barely slept. I suppose I prayed, but I hardly remember anything.

Day after day, I hoped and prayed that they'd find Samira. Whenever the phone rang I knew it was Samira. She'd giggle and tell me she did run away. And then we'd recite, "Friends forever, friends forever, friends for ever more."

But she never called.

And they never found her.

Ever.

And that Jason person, they never found him either.

They came over my house and happened to bring that picture up from where she downloaded it to look at it, and you know what? Come to find out, that picture belonged to some guy named Christopher Peterson, who had a whole website of his summer vacation, and that's where this "Jason" person got it from. But as for Christopher, he never even heard of Samira. And after a thorough investigation, they found out he was telling the truth.

It's been almost ten years, and I still don't know what happened to Samira. I know what likely happened, but I don't like to go there. Whenever my mind tries to go there, and dig deep into the dark unknown, I stop it, and just hear her voice, "Friends forever, friends forever, friends for ever more."

But it has not been an easy ten years, I'll tell you that. Because nothing's the same. My parents don't trust me, Samira's parents don't trust me, and with good reason, although I wanna scream "Im sorry!" at the top of my lungs. But I don't know if they'd ever forgive me, especially Samira's parents. I mean, I betrayed every trust you can think of. And just to think, I *knew*, O Lord, I *knew* it was wrong. But I let her. I let her! I just watched as she spiraled down this darkness, and I did nothing. Said nothing. Except push her farther.

How shameful. How utterly shameful.

And only Allah knew where my friend was right then.

Now (a brooding sigh). Now, I just lie down sometimes outside in our backyard and stare up at the sky. I'd study the gentle movement of the clouds and the remarkable, beautiful power of the sun, and I'd just think, "Who am I?"

And honestly, I don't know. So I'd shut my eyes and whisper prayers to Allah to help me, b/c one thing this thing taught me is that I wasn't who I thought I was. I was living in theory. In theory I was trustworthy, so I believed it. In theory I was a good Muslim, so I believed it. And—

And...

(sighs)

In theory I was a friend, and I believed it.

And for each one. I was wrong.

Dead wrong.

And all I have now is awful regret. O how awful regret is! I spend so much of my time now mentally torturing myself with, if only if, if only if, if only if…

But it's over and I have to remind myself to not go there. The ink has lifted and the pages have dried.

Samira is gone.

Samira is gone.

Samira is gone.

And although it's hard to accept it. It was I who held her hand and pushed her away, even if gently, and even if shyly, but I pushed her. And as certain as the sun rising each morning I pushed her, if for no other reason than I never told her no.

Drowning
Beneath Her Feet

a five-part short story

"I would drown in the ocean every morning
just by stepping out of bed."
—Casey Renee Kiser, *Snail Vixen and The Crystal Garden*

PART ONE
The Suffocating Cloth on My Head

"You always look as though you think people aren't going to like you — that's your trouble."
— Victoria Holt, *Menfreya in the Morning*

1

I blamed the nail in the wall, at least at first. But that was before it occurred to me that I should blame myself. I should have known things would happen just as she said they would. And that made me angry. And my anger made me ashamed. And my shame made me angry at my shame. But then finally, all of those feelings were swallowed up with self-loathing regret.

"Allah doesn't like girls who displease their parents," I heard my mother say so clearly, it was as if she were sitting right next to me in the passenger seat that late afternoon.

"And what about *boys*?" I muttered in frustration under my breath, something I'd never have done when my mother was alive. Immediately, the pang of self-loathing shame jabbed me in the gut, and I felt sick.

"Astaghfirullah," I said, quickly muttering a prayer, asking God to forgive me. But my heart wasn't in it. I didn't believe Allah would punish me for talking back to a dead woman. But then again, what did I know? Paradise still lay beneath her feet—even if she was no longer here to kick me into that humiliating position whenever I pissed her off.

Instinctively, my right hand went to the cloth on my head as my left hand still gripped the steering wheel. I tugged at the fabric beneath my chin and readjusted it as I glanced quickly in the rearview mirror before returning my eyes back to the road, though I couldn't see much of my hijab in the horizontal reflection.

"Pay attention to your patterns," my therapist kept telling me. "When you feel that self-loathing overwhelm you, what do you do?"

It was a familiar pattern, so I should have been used to it by now. Or at least I should have understood it by now. But I didn't. My pattern was tugging at my hijab or my hair, whichever I could reach first. Sometimes I tugged angrily. Sometimes I tugged gently. Sometimes I tugged mindlessly.

Today was mindless.

That is, until I *realized* I was being mindless.

Then I tugged angrily at the cloth until I felt the scarf pin snap at the side of my head. The car veered just a bit as both of my hands instinctively protected the loosened cloth from slipping from my head. But I quickly returned my left hand to the steering wheel to regain control of the vehicle, then tucked my hijab in place with my right.

At the burial earlier that day, I'd stared at the mounds of dirt surrounding the grave they'd prepared for my father, and I felt a compelling urge to walk over those mounds and settle into the ground myself. It wasn't a deliberate inclination, and it certainly wasn't a comforting one.

When they'd buried my mother in the same Muslim graveyard about three years before, I'd felt nothing at all, except the urge to keep my legs from collapsing from beneath me.

But today, as I drove to the repast that I was still trying to figure out a way to get out of, I wondered at the cold ground of existence that I was doomed to lie on for the rest of my life, curled into a fetal position beneath my mother's calloused feet. I wondered what the imams meant when they said that that's where Paradise lay for me. And I wondered if they'd say the same thing if they'd ever met my mother. She always mocked the imams I quoted from, especially whenever I shared with her something inspirational that had touched my heart.

"But is he African-American?" she'd ask, her tone an air of rebuke and condescension.

Sometimes he was. Sometimes he wasn't. *But what difference does it make?* I'd think, though I knew better than to move my lips to utter this question out loud. But my mother would read my mind anyway. She always did. *How did she do that?*

Or maybe it was my face that communicated to my mother what my tongue never could. I was never good at hiding my feelings. And maybe that was my sin...

"The fact that you don't understand why that matters shows why it matters most. Especially for you," she'd say, as if I were the only Black-American Muslim who enjoyed to the lectures of "foreign" sheikhs. "You're filled with so much self-hate, you don't even realize it. You think it's perfectly fine to let people who look down on you tell you how to feel about your soul. And frankly, Lily, that's just sad."

Tears welled in my eyes at the memory, and a lump developed in my throat. *She's right*, my heart said, falling in submission as I blinked back my tears. No matter how difficult it was to accept it, my mother was right about me. I didn't love myself very much. But it had nothing to do with the sheikhs I listened to. It was her voice I'd hear every time I was reminded of the hopelessness of my life.

My mother had predicted that I'd be alone, unmarried and childless for the rest of my life. And right then, at thirty-three years old, I was well on my way of proving her right. It was true that I wasn't particularly inclined to get married, but still, even if the idea of marriage had appealed to me, who'd want to marry *me*?

"Nobody wants a wife who can't respect the man who's taking care of her," she'd say. "If you don't respect your father, you can never respect your husband. And no man wants to live with some psycho feminist running her mouth all day about how she *feels*."

Whenever my mother would drag out the word "feels" in that sneering singsong manner of hers, I felt all the foolishness of my existence. I felt the foolishness of thinking that my feelings mattered at all, or that they even should. It was dumb to even *hope* to be seen or heard, especially by a man. My job was to sacrifice myself for my parents—and then for my husband—and hope Allah would forgive me for not wanting to.

Perhaps if I'd listened to my mother, I wouldn't have wasted eleven months of my life in a so-called "marriage" that was doomed to fail before it even began. Perhaps I wouldn't have spent nearly every day of that "marriage" burdening Mahmoud with all my tears, frustrations, and hopes in life.

"Mark my words," my mother had said fifteen years ago, just days after my father reluctantly held a small *nikaah* for me and Mahmoud in our family living room, "I prophesize your divorce."

In the end, she was right. I should have known that by the expressions of discomfort on the faces of the two witnesses, whose constant glancing at their watches made it clear that they had somewhere else they'd rather be.

It just hurt to learn that my father had called Mahmoud about six weeks before he divorced me to tell him he should. "If you have any sense," my father had told my husband at the time, "you'd divorce that worthless *bint*."

Bint was the Arabic word for girl, but whenever my father said it, I winced. It always sounded like he was referring to a female dog instead of a human girl, and I hated him for it.

The resentment I held toward my father because of that *bint* analogy was another thing I never allowed myself to admit while my parents were alive, let alone say out loud. But right then, as I pulled my car into the packed parking lot of the masjid where my father had been the head sheikh and imam, I didn't resist the thought, or the resentment.

I just wondered why this dark feeling didn't feel as sinful as the one I'd had about my mother.

PART TWO
Burying Daddy One Last Time

"Lies rob us of our trust and we project our untrustworthiness onto everyone around us. Have you ever noticed that the innocent are very trusting? They neither lie nor hold other people's lies against them."
— Donna Goddard, *Waldmeer*

2

"May Allah be pleased with your father," I heard the voices around me say over and over again until I felt dizzy in frustration and exhaustion. "We seek his love and intercession and ask Allah to let his luminous grave light the way on our path."

"Thank you," I muttered over and over again, feeling a bit of my strength come back each time I uttered those two words. I couldn't bring myself to say "Ameen" to their prayers, their utterances that reeked of *shirk*—paganism. And thank God for that. It was the one thing that I felt I had a right to that day, and I wasn't going to budge on it just because I knew my parents would be disappointed in me. No matter how much I tried to do everything they'd wanted me to, I couldn't contain my disgust at witnessing this spiritual charade that my father had started in the name of religion.

Most of the people there knew that I wasn't part of my father's tariqa, or at least suspected that I wasn't. But their eyes told me that they knew my father had forgiven me for this grave sin—and that they were willing to forgive me too. It was like they knew that my father's death had made me see the error of my ways, so they were welcoming me back.

The mere thought incensed me with rage. How dare my father continue to steal my soul even after Allah had taken his. Couldn't I at least keep my spiritual dignity after all they had taken from me?

"We're going to miss the Sheikh so much," an elderly woman said, pulling me into an unwanted hug and weeping against me until I contemplated pulling away to wipe my face. But I stood still until she'd gotten out all her grieving, unsure of the correct etiquette in this circumstance. I alternated between a sympathetic smile and a sympathetic frown, switching expressions each time I imagined my mother shaking her head in disapproval at my inability to even know what facial expression to use at a time like this.

"He's one of the *awliyaa'* of Allah," my mother would say in exasperation at my audacity to disagree with a single teaching of my father. (By *awliyaa'* she meant "divine saints.") But it was never my intention to oppose him.

At that time so many years ago, I was only seventeen years old, so I'd genuinely had no idea there was anything to legitimately oppose. I was just being a teenager, saying whatever was on my mind. I was so naïve though. I'd had no idea that what the Qur'an taught and what my father taught were two different things.

"How dare you act like you know the Qur'an better than one of Allah's saints!" my mother would say in her signature indignant tone. It was a special tone reserved only for me.

As a teenager and into my early 20's, these were the words that would keep replaying in my mind. These were the words that ultimately propelled me toward studying the Qur'an and prophetic teachings more deeply myself. These were the words that inspired me to actually study what I was reading from Allah's teachings and compare them to what I was hearing from my father's teachings.

The disparity was as shocking as it was painfully obvious.

Why can't they see it too? That's the question I could never quite answer.

Or maybe I was the one refusing to see that they *could* see the obvious disparity but just didn't care.

"Your father was chosen by Allah and sent as the light of humanity to our people!" my mother would say. Her raised voice was intended to convince me of the heartfelt conviction in these words. But I could tell that even she didn't believe them, at least not fully.

My mother's Achilles' heel was her pride. But it was not self-centered pride per se. Rather her pride was in being my father's wife. This was her entire identity, actually. She didn't have a separate identity for herself.

It was like my mother's very life had depended on letting the world (and herself) know that she would always stand by my father's side—that she'd honor this man's saintly legacy to her last breath.

Even when he wasn't behaving saintly.

"It's our duty to honor the man Allah sent to us, speaking the language of our people."

Yet this man who was "sent by God" constantly left his dirt-stained, sweat-dampened socks scattered throughout the house. And that made it all the more difficult for *me* to imagine him as an infallible saint, let alone "the close friend" of Allah they insisted he was.

I'd heard my mother herself—more than once—lose her patience with that "divinely guided man" and snap at him for his carelessness. So, I wasn't buying anything she said about his spiritual infallibility. He binge-watched Netflix like the rest of us—and he often didn't even bother to turn his head when nudity was on the screen. I at least did *that*.

PART THREE
Self-Righteous Denial

"Until you heal your first wounds, everyone else will hurt."
—Ezinne Orjiako, *Nkem*

3

"I think it's time for you to admit you were abused and part of a cult," my therapist said gently, as if I hadn't heard her the first time when she'd mentioned it weeks ago during our appointment.

"You people always want to label everything abuse," I snapped back. My heart raced at the cruelty of my words, and somewhere in my conscious mind I knew I was deflecting rather than face the painful truth of what she'd said. Tears stung my eyes, but I told myself they were due to the rage I felt for her as my therapist, not the heartbreak, helplessness, and grief I felt for myself.

"And look at you," I said, gesturing my hand toward the gold crucifix on her neck, "worshipping a man who looks like Jim Carrey, except with a long hair and a beard." I hmphed. "You're the one walking around with a symbol of a bloody sacrifice on your neck. *That's* a cult."

She was silent, but I could tell my words had cut deep. And that gave me a sense of satisfaction. Now she knew how it felt to be judged.

The rest of the session finished in a blur, leaving me with only flashbacks from my father's repast, an event a didn't want to revisit and a time I didn't want to relive.

"Your father was the light of my soul!" an elderly woman had said, tears welling in her eyes and hand resting on my arm just hours after we'd buried my father. "He really was one of Allah's saints!"

It took everything in me not to slap her hand away. Why did people keep saying that? And based on what exactly? This is the question that gnawed at me as I grabbed a napkin from a nearby table and wiped the elderly woman's tears from the side of my face.

After tossing out the napkin in a trash can, I hung back near the doors as droves of people lined up for food. *Does everyone here really think he was a saint?*

Whenever my mother spoke about my father's sainthood, I always maintained a calm, respectful silence and kept my head bowed. It was a gesture of deference that was meant more to hide my expression of embarrassment on her behalf than to display any sincere humility on my part. I didn't want my mother to see my face well enough to read my mind, as she always seemed to do.

"Lily Sheikh Noor," I heard someone say with such lighthearted ease that I immediately turned my head in the direction of the sound.

The friendly face looked vaguely familiar beneath the patchy beard with coils of gray framing the widening smile. But I couldn't place it with a name. He looked to be in his mid to late forties, too young to be a friend of my father, and too old to be a childhood friend of mine.

"You probably don't remember me," the man said, his amiable presence disarming me.

I felt myself actually exhale, as if the room didn't feel so suffocating anymore. I have no idea why, but the aura of this strange man felt vaguely familiar and made me feel both relieved and at ease.

"I'm Abdur-Rahman Mills," he said. "I used to do security for your father."

"Oh yeah," I heard myself say, laughing in sudden recollection with those words. "I didn't recognize you at first."

I instinctively crossed my hands over my chest, my go-to gesture to keep from shaking hands with men. In my father's tariqa, they believed that physical touch was a means of channeling a spiritual connection between members. Yet to my pleasant surprise, Abdur-Rahman didn't even attempt to touch me.

"I didn't really expect you to," Abdur-Rahman said, and I sensed a trace of disappointment in his voice. He averted his gaze momentarily, then looked at me again. "It's been a while since my services were needed."

At that, I looked away. I rested my eyes on the slowly moving lines of people getting food, distracting myself from the memory of how my father had been bedridden for that last eighteen months of his life. My brother had said it was losing my mother that took away the last bit of strength that my father had had. But I didn't believe that.

The doctors had said that it was my father's cancer spreading rapidly that took away his ability to function normally. And that's what I believed. Because whatever strength he'd lost in his limbs he'd certainly channeled to his voice. Daily, he'd bark orders at me from his bed, and his voice would jar me into alertness, even if I was asleep in my room on the next floor up.

"Over thirty years old and still living with your parents," my father would say in bitter disappointment almost every time I appeared in his doorway to see what he needed. He and I both knew that I'd only moved back home because Mom had died and because his health had deteriorated. If there was any other reason I'd moved back home it was because my brother, Bilal, despite being the eldest, would never sacrifice a single part of his life to help out at home—unless he was getting his name scribbled on a check in return or money transferred directly into his account.

"Is Bilal here?" Abdur-Rahman asked as if on cue, scanning the crowd before returning his attention to me. "I didn't see him at the burial."

I nodded, willing myself not to look around the room for my brother, fearing he'd already made his way to the airport and managed to skip the repast altogether, unlike myself.

"He was there," I offered, remembering my brother standing far away from the gravesite but close enough to the crowd to be counted as dutifully present. "But he might've gone home now."

Abdur-Rahman frowned regretfully. "I wanted to give him my salaams."

"I'll tell him when I speak to him, *inshaa'Allah*," I said, hoping my disappointment with my brother didn't show in my voice. I couldn't believe he hadn't even given *me* salaams before he disappeared. I wondered if he'd spoken to Rose before he left. He and my elder sister always had a close relationship with each other—and with my parents—while I wasn't close to anyone in the family.

Then again, I was the only one who'd made it known I wasn't going to be part of anybody's tariqa, even my own father's. So, that probably explained why I wasn't exactly anyone's first choice in confidants.

Yet still, that hurt. But not as much as joining in their spiritual farce would have. I just couldn't torture myself like that, no matter how much I sometimes *wished* I could, if for no other reason than to win back my parents' love.

"I'm sorry for your loss," Abdur-Rahman said, his voice subdued, as if my sudden melancholic mood reminded him of the gravity of that day. "May Allah forgive him his sins and have mercy on him."

My eyes widened at his unexpected but welcomed words. "Ameen," I said for the first time that day, a question in my tone and expression. I searched Abdur-Rahman's face for the answer to what I knew would be disrespectful to my father's memory to speak out loud.

A hesitant smile creased a corner of Abdur-Rahman's mouth as he instinctively glanced around him, careful that no one else could overhear. "I'm no longer part of the Nooriyah tariqa," he said in a lowered voice, referring to the name given to the tariqa my father had founded.

In my father's tariqa, it was believed that those who'd reached the state of sainthood had no sins to be forgiven, and that their spiritual light (*noor*) could bestow mercy on others after death.

"And you believe he deserves that prayer of forgiveness and mercy?" I blurted, too taken aback by Abdur-Rahman's confession to register that this question was more disrespectful than the one I'd remained silent on moments ago.

I could tell by the expression of disapproval on Abdur-Rahman's face that he didn't like my question. "Look," he said, as if leveling with me, "I don't get into what's going on in people's hearts. I know that a lot of the stuff the Sheikh taught contradicted the Qur'an, but—"

"To say the least," I interjected, my inability to conceal my irritation shocking me.

"—I hope he was just ignorant," Abdur-Rahman said, his words overlapping mine.

I grunted and rolled my eyes, unsure why I couldn't keep quiet. Everything inside me told me to shut up, that now wasn't the time. "Good luck with that one," I said, feeling a surge of anger rising inside me.

Mentally, I tried to force it down, but the words rolled off my tongue before I could stop them. "I shared with my father every *ayah* from the Qur'an that I could to show him he was wrong, but he'd just call me arrogant and say I was possessed by Shaytaan and needed that devil knocked out of me." And by "Shaytaan," my father had meant Lucifer, the chief devil.

My heartbeat quickened as the truth of my words overtook me, and the anger I felt at my father kept rising in waves in my chest. "He wasn't ignorant," I said, my face growing hot. "*That*, he was not, I can assure you."

Abdur-Rahman turned away, glancing awkwardly about the room, as if fearing others might overhear.

"He didn't want to hear *anything* from the Qur'an," I vented, "and he didn't want to hear anything from *me*."

"Lily…" Abdur-Rahman interjected, his voice low but firm as he raised a hand to stop me. But for some reason, I couldn't stop myself.

"So, let's just hope that *I'm* the one who's ignorant, and that this so-called saint everybody is here to praise and honor for his spiritual *perfection* has a shot at even a *grain* of Allah's forgiveness and mercy. Though I'm sure, if he could speak from the grave, he'd scoff at even *that* thought."

PART FOUR

Insomnia

"The beautiful thing about the past is that it is in the past, and we never have to go back there again. We can go there in our thoughts to extract lessons, but we never have to be there again. God is so Merciful in what He has given us.
We have now, and we have possibilities."
—Jamilah El-Amin

4

I spent the night alternating between crying uncontrollably and struggling to catch my breath. I knew it was just an anxiety attack, but I feared I would die from this one. It felt like my heart would burst for the humiliation I felt right then. My mind kept replaying my conversation with Abdur-Rahman

Finally, by some miracle, I lay away in the quiet loneliness of the otherwise empty house. I felt like an intruder in the place I'd called home since childhood.

Why wasn't I somewhere running a business or something? Why hadn't I sought escape like Rose, tucking myself away in an environment of plush indifference offered by a hotel on this fateful day that we'd buried my father? Why didn't it occur to me that this house and bed were too invested in my father's legacy to let me sleep?

I wondered what I was even doing here. I didn't belong in this house. Why then had *both* my parents agreed that I should be the one to own it after they passed away? Was this their way of guilting me, one last time, into feeling obligated to give up my life for them?

I hated myself for thinking it. But the more I considered the possibility, the more it made sense. Why else would their two obvious favorites be skipped over in such a significant inheritance?

"We need you to take care of the house when we're gone," my mother had said one day, weeks after we all knew she was terminally ill. "And Lily," she said, her tone rising, as if preparing to scold me for the hesitation she knew I was feeling, "it's the least you could do."

I didn't realize until my mother had passed away and my father was gravely ill himself that this meant that I would be the sole legal owner of the property. But by then, it was discussed as if it was the height of privilege and honor. So, I'd swallowed every question I had and suppressed every flicker of discomfort I felt.

I woke up when the light of dawn glowed bright behind my window blinds, announcing that I had only about fifteen minutes before sunrise. I scrambled out of the bed and rushed to perform *wudhoo'* (ablution) and pray Fajr in time.

In the bathroom, as the grogginess of sleep wore off, I recalled that I'd dreamed about that nail in the wall again. As usual, the nail had been ripping the cloth of my *khimaar*, my favored hijab that I so often wore for prayer and when running errands outside the house.

When I got dressed that morning, having agreed to meet Abdur-Rahman for coffee, the cloth of my hijab actually *did* get snagged by a nail on the wall. It ripped a wide hole in it.

That was when I blamed the nail.

That was also when I yanked the frayed *khimaar* from my head and left the house as if nothing was missing.

PART FIVE
Breaking and Drowning

"Sometimes we just have to sit with the pain for a bit and not rush ourselves to find the lesson, silver lining, or expansive take away. Yes, it's there, but it's also not going anywhere. We don't have to prolong suffering, but we also don't always have to rush healing. There is information to being present to every stage.
—Vienna Pharaon (via Instagram @mindfulmft)

5

I never put my hijab back on again.

At least not for some time.

Instead, I walked out the house that day bareheaded and never returned to that house again. And after my last scheduled appointment with my therapist, I never returned to that city.

I never did meet Abdur-Rahman for coffee either. I never even spoke to him again after that.

It took me only a month of spiritual rebellion before that very same deep, dark emptiness that had pushed me away from Allah compelled me to start praying Salaah again. But it took another three years before I could bring myself to publicly identify as a Muslim or wear hijab.

And whenever anyone asked what happened during that time of spiritual darkness, I told them about the nail on the wall. I spoke of that tiny pieced of rusted metal wedged into the wall as if its very existence had been the final straw for me—instead of my father dying in spiritual darkness himself.

But I was determined to honor his memory. And my mother's, too.

So, I never got married again.

This is the way I looked at it. That was the *one* wish of theirs that I could honor in their name. So, yes, I could play the role my mother had prophesized for me—that of the pitiful divorced woman. Thus, in front of our community and the rest of the world, I made sure I showed up as they imagined me—"bitter, unhappy, and alone"—even long after all traces of bitterness and unhappiness left me.

No, it wasn't the truth, and it wasn't fair. But I felt that my accepting being perceived that way by others was a just recompense (punishment?) for not taking their spiritual path.

I decided to keep the truth between just me and God: that I was *happier* alone. I told myself it was a way of honoring my parents to let family, friends, and loved ones think that I was chronically lonely and "missing out." They needed to feel superior to me, and that was a feeling I was happy to give them.

However, deep inside, I was just thankful to have one less obligatory sacrifice to make in this world. I was just happy to have one less life of misery.

Quite frankly, I was mentally exhausted and emotionally spent. I was so sick and tired of having to suppress my voice, to disappear myself from existence, and to pretend that my thoughts and feelings didn't matter. All in the name of honoring someone else, someone who likely wouldn't believe he had to make a single sacrifice for me.

I was so over it.

I had been there and done that—and I wasn't at all impressed with the experience.

Thank God I don't have to do that *anymore,* I thought to myself.

Thank God!

Read FREE Books by Umm Zakiyyah

About the Author

Known for her soul-touching books and spiritual reflections on emotional healing, Umm Zakiyyah is a world-renowned author, speaker, and soul-care mentor. She specializes in supporting women of faith transform into the best version of themselves—personally, emotionally, and spiritually.

Also known by her birth name Ruby Moore and her "Muslim name" Baiyinah Siddeeq, Umm Zakiyyah is the internationally acclaimed, award-winning author of more than fifty books, including novels, short story collections, and self-help. Her books are used in high schools and universities in the United States and worldwide, and her work has been translated into multiple languages.

Her novel *His Other Wife* is now a short film (available on Prime Video).

Umm Zakiyyah is certified in Rapid Transformational Therapy ® (RTT) and hypnotherapy, qualifications she earned under the guidance of Marisa Peer, author of *I Am Enough*. She also holds a certificate in trauma and somatics.

Umm Zakiyyah studied Arabic, Qur'an, Islamic sciences, *'aqeedah,* and *tafseer* in the USA, Egypt, and Saudi Arabia for more than fifteen years.

Umm Zakiyyah has a BA degree in Elementary Education, an MA in English Language Learning, and Cambridge's CELTA (Certificate in English Language Teaching to Adults).

She is currently based in Dallas, Texas (USA).

Connect with her online:
UZ books: uzauthor.com

Feminine Soul Reset: sqsoul.com
Our Beautiful Qur'an Journey: uzhearthub.com
Instagram/TikTok: @uzauthor
Email: uz@uzauthor.com